THE DOUGLASES

BRETHREN OF THE COAST

BARBARA DEVLIN

This is a work of fiction. Names, characters, organizations, places, events, and incidents are either products of the author's imagination or are used fictitiously.
Copyright © 2014 Barbara Devlin
All rights reserved.
No part of this book may be reproduced, or stored in a retrieval system, or transmitted in any form or by any means, electronic, mechanical, photocopying, recording or otherwise, without the express written permission of the publisher.
Published by Barbara Devlin
The Brethren of the Coast Badge is a registered trademark ® of Barbara Devlin.
Cover art by Wicked Smart Designs
Ebook ISBN
Print ISBN: 978-1-945576-00-3

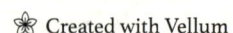

❀ Created with Vellum

LOVING LIEUTENANT DOUGLAS

*This book is dedicated to my wonderful readers, the Nautionniers.
You are the reason I write, and I am so grateful for you.*

CHAPTER ONE

London
November, 1785

"I think dancing with a military man quite unworthy of you," commented an anonymous disparager.

"Oh, I could not agree more." An unknown female snickered. "Why on earth would any woman consider a soldier or a sailor, when there are so many eligible, titled targets in our midst?"

Given the unforgivable slight by the unseen snobs, Royal Navy Lieutenant Mark Douglas of the HMS *Boreas* stiffened his back, leashed his temper, and seethed in silence. He peered over his shoulder, spied a wealth of distinctive auburn curls, partially shielded by a large floral arrangement sitting atop a pedestal, but could gain no unobstructed sight, in light of the crush of society misses in his vicinity. In an effort to identify the mean-spirited harridans, and ensure he wasted no time on such flighty fools, he navigated the chasmal ballroom to secure a better vantage, as he could not confront them.

How dare the witless society chits, regardless of pedigree,

cast such unfavorable insults on the brave souls responsible for safeguarding their liberty, so they might spend their night circling the Northcote's polished floor in their frivolous endeavors? He'd wager his last boon they would sing another tune were they privy to his bank balance. Nodding acknowledgments to various notable members of the *ton*, he bade his time to avoid rousing suspicion, because he could not simply demand satisfaction, until the offending debutantes came into full view.

Three young ladies, though he would argue otherwise, based on their slur against his chosen, honorable occupation, sheltered in the shadow of the large pedestal, which supported a crystal vase filled with a fall mix of hothouse roses. What a compelling contradiction. Of the debutantes, including the telltale redhead, he found two unremarkable, but their friend he thought inexpressibly striking.

With locks as black as a crow's feather, the face of an angel, and shimmering eyes as blue as the Mediterranean, the beauty commanded countless admirers, evidenced by the unfortunate pups circling her skirts. An indigo velvet gown encased her siren silhouette, which contrasted with her skin of pure alabaster. How sad it was that such flawless perfection masked an unattractive heart.

In that instant, she met his stare, and a shiver of awareness traipsed his spine. Summoning years of well-honed polite civility, and refusing to stoop to her level, he dipped his chin. And then she smiled. An imaginary but nonetheless powerful bolt of lightning seared his gut, the walls collapsed, the crowd vanished into thin air, the candlelight dimmed, the music faded into the background, and the world rocked beneath his feet.

To his relief, she appeared unaffected and lost interest, when she bent her head and addressed her cohorts. But to his unmitigated horror, she departed her accomplices in nefarious enterprises and steered in his direction. Myriad introductions fogged

Loving Lieutenant Douglas

his brain, as he searched for a suitable rejoinder, one that would spare him the humiliation of begging a waltz, which he knew she would refuse.

When a lobster, and a mere second lieutenant, at that, executed a brilliant flanking maneuver, Mark sighed and rolled his shoulders, in an effort to alleviate the tension investing his frame. Poor bastard had no idea of the barracuda lurking in inhospitable waters. To his infinite surprise, the raven-haired goddess acquiesced. Just what was she about?

Loitering on the edge of the dance floor, he studied the fascinating creature for the better part of an hour, as she indulged a veritable legion of uniformed admirers, regardless of rank. With a cherubic countenance, she shared conversation and seemed genuinely attentive to her litany of partners, and he could not tolerate it.

"She is lovely, is she not?"

"I beg your pardon?" Mark started and then stood tall. "Captain Randolph, sir. And how are you this fine evening?"

"My arse smarts, my knees ache, and my belly hurts." The legendary seaman Brent Randolph chuckled. "But my wife is happy, and that is all that matters."

"Oh, I say." He winced. "Is that the way the wind blows in the marital state?"

"It does, if you hope to retain your sanity. A happy wife means a happy life. Of course, one must be more than a little insane to willingly don the preacher's noose." Randolph rubbed his neck. "But if you ever breathe a word of that to my Beth, I will kill you."

"Am I interrupting anything of importance, Captain?"

Mark turned to discover none other than the source of his discomfit, and his blood pooled in a particularly potent six inches of his anatomy when he met the gorgeous specimen of the fairer sex in dangerously close proximity.

Randolph sketched a bow. "Lady Amanda—"

"*Just* Lady Amanda, if you please." She cast a flirty pout. "And perhaps I could trouble you for an introduction, Captain Randolph. Who is this estimable lieutenant in our undeserving company?"

Puzzled by her peculiar behavior, which ran contrary to her deprecating remarks, Mark remained a silent spectator. Had she found sport in her rejections? Had she reveled in her victim's anguish?

The captain grimaced. "But your father—"

"Bother my father." She giggled, a lilting sound that kissed his flesh. "And if you do not tell him, neither will I."

"Very well, but if my wife gives me strife for corrupting you, I shall exact recompense." Captain Randolph arched a brow. "Lady Amanda, may I present First Lieutenant Mark Douglas, of His Majesty's Navy and the HMS *Boreas*."

"So happy to make your acquaintance, First Lieutenant Douglas." She half-curtseyed and then averted her gaze. "Is that a waltz? I am quite enamored of it."

And then she stared him straight in the eye. For a minute, they squared off as two opponents on the battlefield. She had thrown down the gauntlet, and he contemplated his next move. Oh, she was a manipulative charmer—one he might not resist were he unaware of her true nature. But before he could respond, Randolph elbowed Mark in the ribs. Against his better instincts, he surrendered. "It would be my honor, Lady Amanda."

Taking her hand in his, Mark led his stunning nemesis to the dance floor. As they assumed their respective positions, with his arm anchored at her waist, which he resolved not to enjoy, he fixed his attention on her crown of ebony ringlets and vowed to offer her the most refined experience of the night. With an elegant flourish, he whirled and carried her with him.

"You serve Captain Nelson?"

"Yes."

"And how is that?"

"Fine."

"Do you favor the Northcote's ball?"

"No."

"Are you not partial to social events?"

"Sometimes."

"You may address me as Amanda, if you wish." She squeezed his fingers. "And what shall I call you?"

"Lieutenant Douglas."

"Have I done something to offend you?"

"I do not know." Daring her to admit the truth, he peered at his not-so-nice partner. "Have you?"

"But—we have only just met." With an expression of unutterable confusion, she blinked. "It was rather forward of me to insert myself into your conversation with Captain Randolph, but I meant no harm."

"Then you are innocent." Her denial spiked his anger, and he bit his tongue against a rapier retort.

"If you have no prior commitment, perhaps you will consent to accompany me to dinner, later. You can share tales of your travels and regale us with your bravery." She looked so hopeful, he almost felt sorry for her—almost. "There is plenty of room at my table."

"No, thank you." Although it was not wise to cut a member of the peerage or their offspring, he enacted a rare breach of decorum, and pride surged to the fore, when her mouth fell agape. It was nothing less than she deserved. The music ended, and he halted. "Allow me to return you to—"

"That is not necessary, as I have intruded on your hospitality long enough." Lady Amanda wrenched from his hold. "Pray, forgive me, *Lieutenant Douglas*."

"Lady Amanda, this is a treat." A sub-lieutenant, which Mark had not recognized, bowed and claimed her attention. "Wait until my wife discovers your presence. She will be overset with joy, as we owe you a debt we can never repay."

"Nonsense, as I did nothing more than bring together two people who love each other. And you should take me to Jane, at once, as I long to see her." She gave Mark her back. "By the by, how is your brother?"

"John is recovered, and he favors the scarf you knitted." The soldier blushed, and Mark was embarrassed for the poor sap. "I understand your singular efforts have resulted in a substantial contribution to the Navy Widows Benevolence Fund."

Again the curious noblewoman befuddled Mark, as her queries belied indifference, and he glanced left and then right. Something was wrong. Despite what he had heard, all was not as it appeared, and he needed an explanation. When he spied Captain Randolph, he stomped to the veteran naval man's side. "Captain, please excuse my intrusion, but I require your assistance."

"Oh, no." Randolph smirked. "I know that look, and you have it bad."

"I beg your pardon?" Mark shuffled his feet. "Just what do you infer?"

"You are smitten with Lady Amanda." Randolph winked and grinned. "Worry not, young Douglas, as your secret is safe with me. But I would not want to be in your boots when you speak with the admiral."

Mark's blood ran cold. "What admiral?"

"Ah, yes. Your ladylove neglected to share her identity with you, and I cannot imagine why." The captain burst into laughter. After an interminable fit of hilarity, he slapped Mark on the back. "Lady Amanda is the youngest daughter of *Admiral* Hiram Gascoigne-Lake, Marquess de Gray."

And Mark's goose was well and truly cooked.

∼

ADOPTING A STIFF UPPER LIP, as her father had taught her, in the face of adversity, or in her case monumental disappointment, Lady Amanda Gascoigne-Lake forced a smile as she partnered a soldier and ignored the abridgment of his military accomplishments, all intended to induce an introduction to her father. As the daughter of an admiral with equally estimable peerage, her connections proved an irresistible enticement to the shameless social climber, and of that there were many, much to her chagrin. So it was a rare occasion, indeed, when she found a marine or a sailor with no prior knowledge of her familial ties.

When she completed the third rotation of the quadrille, the impeccable but impudent Lieutenant Douglas loomed at the edge of the crowd, gazing on her as if he knew how she looked in her chemise, and she missed her step. What an insufferable buffoon.

Resplendent in his regimentals, the handsome naval officer stood at well over six feet, as a veritable mountain of a man—not that she cared. With thick chestnut hair, which he kept close-cropped, austere, chiseled features, a patrician nose, and a pair of the bluest azure eyes, which simmered with naughty thoughts, he claimed her attention to the detriment of all else. But when he cast her a lazy smile, which he had done just then, her heart skipped a beat, her insides flip-flopped, and she crashed into Lady Beth.

"Oh, my. I am so sorry." Amanda cursed the burn of a blush. "How clumsy of me." She resumed her respective position and completed the sequence of moves with nary a blunder.

"Thank you for the honor, Lady Amanda." The officer cadet bowed. "Shall I escort you to your father—"

"May I have the pleasure of the waltz, Lady Amanda?" The new bane of her existence presented for her inspection, and rejection traipsed the tip of her tongue.

"Of course, Lieutenant Douglas." Silly ridiculous fool. Could he not understand the significance of a second accompaniment at the ball? Was he oblivious to etiquette? Polite society would misinterpret his actions as a declaration, regardless of intent, and she should save him from himself and the embarrassment. "I should be too delighted."

With his hand at her waist, and their fingers twined, they whirled beneath the elegant crystal chandeliers. How close he held her, and her skirts brushed his thighs, but Amanda refused to meet his stare. Yet she felt the heat of his scrutiny, as the rising sun on a clear summer morning.

"I see you have a taste for military men." He added insult to injury. "Do you dance attendance to please your father?"

Ah, that explained his change of heart and reflected poorly on his reputation. The lieutenant had discovered her true identity, and now he considered her worthy of his courtesy. Had he presumed her a simpleton, that he could so easily dupe her? Well he knew not with whom he tangled. Recalling their earlier conversation, and his one-word replies, she decided to respond, in kind. It was, for her, a rare breach in decorum, but she cared not for his opinion. Let him enjoy a taste of his own medicine. "Perhaps."

"I notice your fellow debutantes do not share your enthusiasm for the uniform."

"No."

"It would seem they favor titled gentlemen."

"Quite."

"As your father is both, is it safe to presume you more amenable?"

"Indeed."

"Amanda—"

"*Lady* Amanda, if you please."

"But you made me free with your name."

"I rescind such informalities, as our acquaintance is limited, and I have no intention of furthering our connection." She sniffed. Yes, hers was bad form, but in light of his pejorative assessment of her character, she thought herself entitled to a measure of retribution.

"I suppose I deserve that, and I intend otherwise." He chuckled. "Given my earlier behavior, I should apologize. And I wonder if I might reconsider your gracious offer to accompany you to dinner?"

She opened her mouth and then closed it, as a brilliant idea shot to the fore. So the high and mighty lieutenant wanted nothing to do with Lady Amanda but was more than willing to play nice with the admiral's daughter? "*Weeell*, Lieutenant Douglas—"

"Call me Mark," he said with a wink.

"As you wish." Amanda found her feet and resolved to gain her revenge. "I should be uncontrollably excited for you to dine with me."

As if on cue, the bell sounded.

"Shall we?" How charming was her escort.

Strolling amid the sea of couples, Amanda heeded the none-too-silent whispers and pointed gestures, evidencing the *ton* had noted her most recent prospective suitor. Nearing her table, she spied her usual co-conspirator and set course for vengeance. She would teach Lieutenant Douglas a well-earned lesson in manners, and he would think twice before toying with her heart again.

"Cousin Helen, may I introduce Lieutenant Mark Douglas, of His Majesty's Navy." Amanda caught Helen's gaze. "The brave sailor has consented to share his esteemed company with the unworthy."

Mark started. "Amanda, I am undeserving of such acclaim—"

"Oh, I disagree." Helen lowered her chin and grinned. "If my relation deems you unimpeachable, then you have more than earned your just reward, Lieutenant."

And so Amanda abandoned her errant charge to the exceedingly eccentric but reliable thirty-three-year-old, self-professed permanent spinster of the Gascoigne-Lakes. Ever since Amanda's coming out, unscrupulous ne'er-do-wells seeking easy access to the upper stratum of society had besieged her. At first, she quite basked in the attention, given her naïveté and misplaced faith in the male sex. But as she matured to the ripe age of eight and ten, a confidence-gnawing premonition haunted her slumber, until the self-doubt consumed even her waking hours. Over time, a lingering question for which she had no answer had cast a pall over her heart and mind.

Could no one love her for herself?

So she spent the better portion of her days knitting scarves, which she sold to help support navy widows. It was a modest charity, including about sixty society ladies, but it gave Amanda a sense of purpose, when the superficial trivialities and false facades of the peerage shrouded her spirits in a miasma of deceit.

At that instant, Helen's boisterous mirth broke Amanda's reverie. To her amazement, Mark and Helen had their head's together, as two conspiring pranksters. Mark whispered in her ear, and Helen burst into laughter. How could that be, given Helen's understanding of Amanda's wishes? They had struck a bargain. Amanda quarried her prey, and Helen delivered the fatal blow.

"Lady Amanda, I took the liberty of fetching a plate of pork and apples." Samuel Clarendon, a particularly persistent Second Lieutenant in the British Army, claimed the seat beside her without asking permission.

"How very presumptive of you, Lieutenant Clarendon." She wrinkled her nose, as her appetite had waned the second he opened his mouth and with good reason. Braced for the impending assault, she stiffened her spine.

"How many times must I remind you, Lady Amanda?" The grasping schemer had the nerve to rest his arm on the back of her chair. "You must call me Sam. And I should dearly love to be free with your name."

"You are too bold, sir." She had a sneaking suspicion he endeavored to be free with much more than her name, and she was in no mood to indulge him. "But I thank you for the food."

"I have no use for your gratitude, Lady Amanda." He leaned near, and she almost choked on his foul breath, which reeked of a putrid combination of cheap brandy, stale cigars, and spoiled milk. "Have you spoken with your father concerning my platoon assignment?"

"You forget yourself, Lieutenant Clarendon." She scooted her chair to the right. "As I told you, I do not presume to meddle in my father's affairs, as I lack military experience."

"But one word from you could make my career, gentle lady, as I simply must command the Royal Marines aboard Captain Nelson's *Boreas*. You do wish me to promote, do you not, as we are so close to an understanding?" The scoundrel made an improper advance, and she stood before he cornered her into a compromising position. "No doubt your father could plead my cause."

"I know of no understanding, sir, and why would you want to sail on the *Boreas*?" She recalled that was Mark's ship. "Does it signify?"

"Oh, yes." Clarendon pursued her, even as she retreated a

step. "Only the best serve Nelson, and I should be counted among his ranks. If you—"

"Amanda, I need you." Helen snapped her fingers. "You simply must come here, at once."

"I beg your pardon, Lieutenant Clarendon." Amanda dipped her chin. "But family calls."

With anger-driven tears threatening, she all but flew into her cousin's safe haven. As would a gentleman, Mark vacated his seat, which he offered to Amanda. "Thank you, Lieutenant Douglas."

"You are most welcome." To her surprise, Mark stood at attention. "And may I sit beside you, Lady Amanda?"

"Please, do so." How polished were his manners, compared to Clarendon's. "But this is your plate."

"You did not eat, Lady Amanda." Mark inclined his head and frowned. "Shall I collect your meal, or would you prefer a sweetmeat?"

"How very thoughtful you are, Lieutenant." Amanda sighed in relief, as she needed his kindness just then. "I would favor a Shrewsbury cake and, perhaps, a glass of champagne, if it is not too much trouble."

"It is no trouble at all, my lady." He smiled, and her heart skipped a beat. "I shall return, fair Helen. And you should share the events of your recent hunting expedition with your cousin, if you have not done so."

"What an impressive specimen," gushed Helen, after Mark traveled beyond earshot. "He listened to my complaints of gout with a great sum of compassion and suggested a shipboard remedy. What offense did he commit to land him in my trap?"

"Oh, do not be fooled, Helen." Amanda sneered. "He was unforgivably rude until he discovered my parentage."

"No. I do not believe you." Helen appeared crestfallen. "You must be mistaken, as he was a vast deal more than civil, even when I detailed the pain in my big toe."

"Would that I were." In minutes, Amanda described the first waltz with Lieutenant Douglas, his shabby treatment, and his original refusal to dine with her. "And I thought him the first viable candidate of the Little Season. It was humiliating, Helen."

"But what do you suppose caused him to behave in such a crude fashion?" Helen tapped her cheek. "When he has been the soul of genteel congeniality?"

"I know not." Amanda shrugged. "But thank you for rescuing me from Clarendon."

"The shameless blackguard." Helen curled her lip. "He is so low that when he passes to the hereafter, the gravediggers will have to dig up to lay the bastard to rest."

"*Cousin.*" Despite propriety, Amanda giggled. "Dearest Helen, what would I do—"

"And here is your Shrewsbury cake and champagne, Lady Amanda." Mark set the requested items on the table and slid to his seat. "So what are you fine ladies whispering about, or have I interrupted a matter of great importance and secrecy?"

"Actually, I believe you can relate to our conversation, Lieutenant Douglas." She had almost forgotten about her erstwhile suitor, yet her disappointment chilled her to the marrow.

"Oh?" He shifted his weight. "Do tell, my lady."

Amanda caught him in her sights. "We were discussing men with nefarious motives."

CHAPTER TWO

*T*wo days later, Mark brought his curricle to a halt before the London residence of the Marquess de Gray. Built in the Palladian style, the grand home boasted an impressive portico, the highlight of which was an ingress façade featuring a pediment with a tympanum sculpture by Sir Robert Taylor, supported by six Corinthian columns. Only one thing could entice him to visit such an imposing structure. In short, Lady Amanda held court that afternoon.

"First Lieutenant Mark Douglas to see Lady Amanda." He handed his card to the butler.

"Of course, sir." The manservant bowed. "This way, please."

At a double-door entry, a mature woman loomed as an imposing sentry, and she bore a striking resemblance to his lady. "And what have we here?"

"First Lieutenant Mark Douglas for Lady Amanda, your ladyship." The butler presented Mark's card.

"We meet at last, First Lieutenant, and the mystery is solved." She dipped her chin. "I am Lady Eleanor, Marchioness de Gray and Lady Amanda's mother."

"Lady Eleanor, it is an honor." He stood at attention, as he wished to make a good impression. "I am but an undeserving member of Lady Amanda's legion of callers."

"And you are the young man who upset my daughter at the Northcote's ball." Lady Eleanor arched a brow, even as she chuckled. "She speaks of little else, so I must assume you had quite an effect on her."

In that instant, Mark almost revisited his lunch. "My lady, I am truly—"

"Relax, First Lieutenant, as you do not disappoint." To his infinite surprise, the marchioness patted his cheek. "My Amanda is notoriously picky when it comes to her suitors, and she is also ruthless with her admirers, so she would not have mentioned you had you made no favorable influence."

"Indeed." Mark breathed a sigh of relief and pocketed that gem of information for future reference. "May I see her?"

"Oh, yes." Again, Lady Eleanor stunned him, when she clutched his arm and marched him into the fray. "I shall announce you, myself, as I would not miss this for the world."

"Your eyes are like limpid pools of new fallen rain. Upon my heart they have etched a permanent stain." A clumsy oaf dressed in gentleman's attire postulated from the center of the drawing room, as Amanda, with an expression of terminal boredom, reclined at one end of a sofa and yawned. "And your teeth are of the purest white. I should—"

"What an original oratory, Lord Stein. And so refined." The marchioness cleared her throat. "My daughter has another caller. Please, welcome First Lieutenant Mark Douglas to our humble gathering."

A sea of chairs, occupied by an estimated twelve prospective swains, littered the comfortable drawing room, which boasted oak paneling with leather inserts. And both branches of the military, as well as the peerage, were well represented.

"Lieutenant Douglas." Amanda snapped to attention,

leaped from the couch, and all but bounced as she met him. With a glowing smile, she half-curtseyed. Just as quick, she masked her enthusiasm behind an imperturbable visage, which might have succeeded had she not trembled. Oh, she was a veritable spitfire. "It is unfortunate there are no open seats, as you are late."

"Lady Amanda, you are more exquisite than I remembered." He grasped the hand she had not offered, pressed a chaste kiss to her gloved knuckles, and smiled when gooseflesh covered the skin bared by her short-sleeved dress. "A thousand pardons for my oversight."

"Humph." She sniffed. "And what have you there?"

"Roses." He inclined his head. "A meager offering to your beauty."

"My favorite." She accepted the bouquet and buried her nose in a delicate bud. "They are lovely."

"They are but flowers." He shifted his weight to conceal his discomfit, as the woman worked on him in ways he could not have anticipated, and his Jolly Roger had just run up the colors. "You are lovely."

"Mama, will you have these put in water and set them on my bedside table?" She met his gaze for a scarce second and then winced. "Given the other serviceable pedestals are already taken."

"Of course." Lady Eleanor glanced at Mark and winked.

"And what is in the parcel?" Amanda bit her lip, and he fought the urge to taste her.

"Ah, yes." He sketched an elegant bow and presented her with the box. "A modest token of my affection, Lady Amanda."

With unchecked vigor and a squeal of delight, she plopped on the sofa in what he suspected was for her a rare breach in feminine deportment. Again, she reversed course, stiffened her back, and presumed an air of ennui, which had not fooled him for a minute. "I suppose you may sit beside me, Lieutenant Douglas, as it is the only vacancy, due to your astonishing lack of punctuality."

"My sincerest apologies, that I should neglect you, Lady Amanda." He clamped his tongue to keep from laughing, settled at her left, and studied her profile. "Perhaps my gift will persuade you to accept my expressed regret."

"We shall see." With that, she lifted the lid, parted the brown paper, and her icy chill melted before his eyes. "Oh, how charming."

"What is it?" a perturbed potential paramour probed.

"Will you help me, Mark? As I would not damage it for anything in the world." It had not escaped him that she used his first name, in what polite society deemed a shocking display of intimacy, even as he grasped the edges of the container, so she could retrieve the item. "It is the *Boreas*."

A miniature, exact replica of his ship, complete with sails, rested in her palm. She turned it left and then right, before peering at him with the softest, sweetest angelic countenance.

"You serve Nelson?" a lobster inquired, and Mark recognized the chap.

"I am Captain Nelson's first lieutenant." Mark recalled the soldier was, in fact, the very same man from whom Helen had rescued Amanda at the Northcote's ball. "And I do not believe we are acquainted, sir."

"I am Second Lieutenant Samuel Clarendon." The unshaven, rumpled reprobate clicked his heels. "You should remember me to your captain, as my family is well-known in loftier circles, and such mention would be to your credit."

"Thank you, Lieutenant Clarendon, for your generous offer." Mark nodded an acknowledgement, even as he ached to smite the rogue's costard. "But I make my own way."

"I would wager you do." The miscreant attempted to smooth

a wrinkled cuff, even as he delivered a clumsy insult, neither facetious nor serious.

"You may depend upon it." Mark stared the louse straight in the eye until the coward flinched. "Nelson's men do their duty."

"Well, of course." Clarendon coughed into a handkerchief. "And I must away, Lady Amanda. Need to prepare for the Promenade, you know."

As an awkward armada, of sorts, his competitors cast off, but Mark lingered in their wake, until he alone remained in the drawing room. With patience that should qualify him for sainthood, he tamped his temper, while the would-be-wooers made their farewells. At long last, Lady Amanda returned, and she started when she discovered him.

"Lieutenant Douglas, I did not know you were still here." She glanced over her shoulder and then faced him.

"I preferred it when you called me Mark, and I must speak with you about an urgent matter." He chuckled, held out his hands, and flicked his fingers in entreaty. Nonplussed, he swallowed hard when she rested her palms to his, without reservation. "Lady Amanda, I owe you an explanation and an apology for my unforgiveable behavior at the Northcote's ball."

"Oh?" She furrowed her brow. "I had thought, perhaps, my connections swayed your partiality."

"I suppose I deserve that." With his thumb, he traced little circles on her gloved knuckles, and she inhaled a shaky breath, which scored a direct hit to his loins. "But my excuse is no less iniquitous."

"All right." She squared her shoulders. "I will hear you."

"When I first ventured to the Northcote's, I overheard a rather puerile but nonetheless cruel conversation, which cast aspersions on my occupation, but I could not identify the slanderers, beyond a unique characteristic born by one of the young women, for the throng. I knew only that females sheltering near a large pedestal, which bore an imposing floral arrangement, professed the uniform beneath them." He considered his words; as he would not compound his err. "To avoid detection, I navigated the crowd with patience and discretion until I gained an unimpaired view of the detractors, one of whom sported the singular red hair."

"*Lady* Mary Ann and *Lady* Cynthia, although I would argue otherwise." She wrenched from his grasp and paced. "*Vipers*. How dare they?"

Unprepared for the force of her reaction, Mark found her unutterably appealing, and she earned a measure of respect from him, in that instant. "Lady Amanda—"

"Well that explains the hushed whispers and silence with which they met my arrival, as they know better than to spout such venom in my company." Riding a wave of high dudgeon, she whirled about, snorted, and stomped a foot. "My own beloved father is an admiral, and I am a vast deal prouder of his military rank than the peerage, as the one he earned, and the other he gained through birth."

"Well said, my lady." How he loved the fire in her blue eyes and the raw power of her fury. He could only hope that energy lent itself to other, more intimate endeavors. "Perhaps now you can understand—"

"*Oh*. You believe me like-minded?" She gasped, clenched a fist to her bodice, and then his valorous heroine broke. With tears welling, and chin quivering, she said in a small voice, "Do you think so little of me?"

"No." But he deserved a swift kick in the arse. "Lady Amanda, I should—"

"Please, you must call me Amanda." She wiped her cheek, and he cursed himself for making her cry. "If you are going to insult me, I should make you free with my name."

"Sweet Amanda." Oh, she was a diamond of the first water

—one he would neither overlook nor take for granted. He would never know why he had done it, but Mark walked straight to his lady and drew her into his embrace, propriety be damned. "I should sooner cut off my right arm than cause you pain. And yet, however unintended, I have hurt you, and I am so sorry."

"Well, I suppose I can accept your reasoning." When he dabbed her heart-shaped face with his handkerchief, she favored him with a watery, lopsided smile, and he caught his breath. Then and there, Mark vowed she would be his wife. "Though you really should not have leapt to unsupported conclusions woven from whole cloth."

"I am duly chastised." He whisked a stray tendril and tucked it behind her ear. "And if it makes you feel any better, the injury I caused you is nothing compared to the wound I have inflicted upon myself."

"Lieutenant Douglas—"

"—Mark."

"Oh, Mark." She giggled. "Cousin Helen is correct in her estimation. You are an impressive specimen, though I would add dangerous to the mix."

To wit he burst into laughter. "And I would say the same of you, my Amanda."

In that moment, she positively glowed. "And am I your Amanda?"

"If only you allow me the opportunity to set things right between us." He had not realized he searched for a mate when he had entered the Northcote's residence, but he was too smart to pass on a golden opportunity, when she so audaciously upbraided his questionable conduct. Yes, indeed, she would be his bride, because when Mark wanted something, he claimed it. And he wanted Amanda. "So what would you ask of me, that I may be your Mark?"

Loving Lieutenant Douglas 25

"My dearest Lieutenant, you were mine from the moment I saw you." And now she emanated inexpressible joy. "And while I do love the replica and the roses, I have a couple of commissions, which would absolve you of your past transgressions, and we should never mention them again if you succeed."

"You have only to ask." Though the etiquette books frowned on such behavior, Mark tugged off one of her gloves and pressed his lips to her bare palm. For several minutes, they simply stared at each other, as passion shimmered in the air as a gentle spring shower. Then he bent his head, and she tipped her chin—

From beyond the drawing room, a lady cleared her throat.

"Mama waits in the hall." Amanda touched his mouth with a finger, and he caught it between his teeth in a playful nip. When he winked, she clucked her tongue, retreated a step, and settled her skirts. "First, you must purchase one of my hand-knitted scarves, in support of the Navy Widows Benevolence Fund, and you must encourage your shipmates to do the same. And although I have never seen you at the Promenade, I would have you escort me, this afternoon, with my cousin Helen as chaperone."

"*My* Amanda, I am most definitely at your service."

~

A FORTNIGHT HAD PASSED, and Amanda fidgeted as she waited beneath the signature oak in Hyde Park, which had become her rendezvous point with Mark, whereupon he never failed to escort her during what she had once considered the morose spectacle known as the Promenade. In fact, their strolls amid society had charged the fore as her most cherished pastime, second only to the waltz, when he held her in his arms and whispered naughty thoughts in her ear. Just thinking of it gave her delicious shivers.

"Oh, where could he be?" With nervous anticipation, she perched on her toes, glanced from side to side, and craned her neck.

Yes, at last, it seemed she had found her knight in shining armor. Not once, in all their assignations, and of that there had been many, had Mark requested an introduction to Papa or suggested she recommend her beau for career advancement. Instead, they shared like-minded hopes for their future, based on identical priorities of family and service. And to his credit, her lieutenant encouraged her charitable work.

"Will you please calm yourself?" Helen chortled. "He will be here, but we are early."

"I know, but I long to see him." And then she made a quick check of her appearance.

The navy pelisse, *á la militaire*, she had designed expressly for her lieutenant's delectation. Composed of rich blue velvet, the garment boasted an arched collar trimmed in Spanish braiding, and three rows of white silk frogs decorated the bodice, which she selected to reflect the piping of Mark's uniform lapels. A brooch and clasps of mother-of-pearl set in old gold fastened the coat at her throat and waist, with a companion bonnet atop her head, and buff kid half boots, with matching gloves, completing the ensemble.

"But you danced three times at the Harris ball, just last night, which makes you the latest *on-dit*." Helen snickered and rocked on her heels. "Everyone is talking, and even your father took note."

"I care not, as I should withhold my attentions exclusive to Mark, had I a choice in the matter." Without thought, she traced the inner side of her wrist and revisited sweet memories of their tryst in the garden at Harris House, when Mark had licked and suckled the sensitive flesh at the base of her hand. To her dismay and disappointment, he had done nothing else. "And regardless of the tenets governing our set, I will not deny what I feel."

"And what do you feel, Lady Amanda?" inquired Mark in a purring tone that bespoke a wealth of meaning she comprehended too well.

"Lieutenant Douglas." Bracing for the sensuous onslaught of her faculties, which always accompanied their initial greetings, she rotated and faced the man of her dreams. Conscious of the multitude stares in their direction she mustered passable aplomb. "What a nice surprise. And how are you this fine day?"

"Indeed, fortune smiles upon me, as I enjoy uncanny good luck." Bedecked in his now familiar blue frock, with a high collar and buttoned cuffs, white pantaloons and stock, polished Hessians, sword, and a cocked hat positioned athwartships he arched a brow. "And, as of this moment, I have never been better."

"Oh, Mark—"

"Ahem." Helen elbowed him in the ribs. "Perhaps you two should start walking, as gout plagues my big toe, and I shall tarry to maintain pace."

"Of course, fair Helen." They shared a conspiratorial glance, as the spinster had pled the same excuse to justify the additional distance she allowed, which stretched the limits of respectability, but Amanda would not complain. Arm in arm, Mark led her into the rotation. "How very nautical you look, Lady Amanda."

"Do you like it?" She smiled and then whispered, "I wore it just for you."

"I shall endeavor not to squander the honor." His chest expanded, as he inhaled, and his muscles tensed beneath her grip when she squeezed him. "And you are quite stunning, if I may be so bold, but you merely put a frame on a masterpiece, my Amanda."

"I do so love it when you call me that." She shuddered and dipped her chin to various notables. "And I am loathe to press your suit, but do you not think it overdue to speak with my father? Should I make the introductions tonight, at the Saumarez's?"

"Are you not the officious little thing?" Amanda's heart sank, even as her beau chuckled and tapped the tip of her nose. "And that is not necessary, because I have already secured your father's permission to pay court."

"What—when?" She stumbled and would have fallen, had he not firmly anchored her at his side. "Why did you not tell me? And when were you planning to impart that important bit of information?"

"Easy, my dear." He tipped his hat to Lady Berkley. "We do not want to feed the gossipmongers."

"My dear Lieutenant Douglas, if you do not enlighten me, I shall scream and land us on the front page of the scandal sheets." She yanked hard on his elbow. "The details—now."

"Ah, you employ that *governessy* tone—what it does for me, my Amanda." He burst into laughter and then covered her hand with his. "My impatient lady, I met your father in the card room, after dinner at the Northcote's, where you executed that adorable if not so efficacious flanking maneuver with Helen, and secured his blessing, which is why I called on you, two days afterward."

"I know not of any such maneuver." She lied and averted her gaze, as it unnerved her that Mark read her with unerring accuracy. "I thought you might find Helen's amity a vast deal entertaining."

"Oh, I did and still do, but she is not half so fascinating as my

Amanda." He bent his head. "And, please, do not bite your lip, as it makes you altogether irresistible."

"Mark, you must not tease me." And then she disobeyed his request before she realized it. "I do so long to kiss you. How I enjoyed our tour of the garden, last night."

"So did I, sweetheart." She thrilled at his declared term of endearment, and when he pinned her with his heated stare, she almost swooned. "But you are temptation personified, lady mine. And I would not compromise you until the banns have been read and the vows spoken."

"What?" Amanda came to an abrupt halt. "Is it too much to hope? Do you intend to—"

"Yes," her maddeningly proper lieutenant replied. "We are on the same page, darling."

"Well you are an odd fellow." And Amanda was overjoyed. "When were you going to apprise me of your objective?"

"At the appropriate time, as I would not make haste and frighten you." He furrowed his brow. "In light of our brief acquaintance, it seemed a wise tack."

"Fie on you, sir, as I do not frighten so easily." She shook with uncontrollable excitement. "But how long have you known?"

"I would wager from the moment I saw you." In an affectation of unimaginable tenderness, he massaged her gloved knuckles with his thumb, as was his way. "You struck a vicious blow from which I may never recover."

"Then more's the pity, for I share your devotion and your affliction." Yet the nagging doubts born of years of abuse by unscrupulous suitors resurfaced. "Can you be certain, given our whirlwind courtship? And I would have the truth."

"Of course, and I know nothing but the truth." He steered her near a large hedge, which provided a modicum of privacy. "My dear, I am a Douglas, and once we fix our minds, we shall not be deterred. I would do well to warn you, that if you have any reservations, you should proclaim them, now. I shall be disappointed, and I may not be kind, but I will not be angry with you. You have my word, as a gentleman, I would abide your preference."

"How could you think me so fickle?" Clasping her hands in his, Mark brought her to face him, and she retreated a fraction to gain a better view, as the crown of her head barely reached his chin. Silly giant. "And I should warn you, that if you renege on your promise, you would do well to remain at sea until the end of your days."

In that instant, her lieutenant looked her in the eyes, and then studied her mouth, before again meeting her stare. And though her coat kept her quite warm, she shivered.

Mark shuffled his feet. "Amanda, I may have to break my oath and claim that kiss, tonight."

"How I wish you would." She licked her lips. "As I ache for you."

"Good God, woman, you make me tremble." He trailed his finger along the curve of her cheek. "I should very much—"

"Well, well, what have we here?" Samuel Clarendon sneered. "The common sailor and rank climber. You should not waste your time, Douglas, as *Lady* Amanda does not oblige, though she does favor the uniform."

"I beg your pardon?" Amanda flinched at the slur.

A chorus of gasps and whispers, which reached a fevered crescendo, given their location in the park, composed a foreboding audial embroidery. And the audience grew as word spread of the slight.

With indefatigable equanimity, which she found indefatigably exasperating, Mark set her at arm's length and bared his teeth. "You will apologize, sir."

"For what?" Clarendon strutted as a peacock, and Amanda

wanted to punch him in the nose. "The lady manipulates us as marionettes on her personal stage, even as she refuses to accommodate us, perhaps because she fears such cooperation might diminish her appeal. But you may play her fool, if you so choose, yet I shall call you on it."

All of a sudden, the crowd parted to permit her father, along with the dodgy-toed Helen, entry to the fray. "What is the meaning of this, Clarendon?"

"I have no quarrel with you, Hiram." The bastard smirked. "At issue is—"

"How dare you address me so informally, as you are neither my equal nor my better?" Amanda's father drew himself up with noble hauteur, and she winced. "I demand satisfaction."

"First you must get in line, Admiral." With his glove, Mark slapped Clarendon across the cheek. "In the name of Lady Amanda Gascoigne-Lake, I challenge you, sir."

Amanda opened her mouth and then closed it. Despite the libel of his character, her magnificent lieutenant took offense not for himself but for her. How glorious was her knight in shining armor? And then the ramifications of Mark's provocation dawned, and she emitted a plaintive cry.

"What?" Clarendon blinked and sputtered.

"You heard me." Stretched to his full height, Mark towered over the blackguard. "Make amends for your affront, retract your aspersions against Lady Amanda's character, or suffer the consequences."

"Mark—no." She stepped forward.

"Quiet, Amanda." Her father yanked her to his side. "Let Douglas handle it."

"Papa, please, do not let him do this." She scanned the immediate area, searching for someone to stop the insanity. Her gallant hero simply could not enact a duel, as she could not marry a corpse, and the mere thought sounded a carillon of gloom. In a flash, an image of herself, garbed in the somber black togs of full mourning, portended doom, and she teetered on the brink of disaster.

"If I slighted anyone, Douglas, it was you." Clarendon spat on the ground at Mark's feet. "What right have you to reparation, when I speak no falseness."

"You have no honor, sir, as you operate under the mistaken presumption that disparagement of my reputation precludes defamation of Lady Amanda." Mark rested hands on hips. "Choose your weapon, and name your second. I will see you at sunrise, on Paddington Green. Be prompt, as you do not want me to come after you."

Amanda shrieked in horror and fainted.

CHAPTER THREE

A nebulous blanket of London fog cast a morbid pall over Paddington Green, while birds chirped a cheery singsong, as a thread of shimmering gold heralded a new day. Mark only hoped it was not his last, as he had plans to make with a certain raven-haired beauty. After a quick assessment of his formal dress uniform, he rolled his shoulders and sighed.

"So you intend to go through with it, Douglas?" Captain Horatio Nelson, Mark's second, shifted his weight and sniffed. "I met your lady last night, at the Saumarez's gala. She is quite handsome."

"Indeed, she is altogether stunning, and I will restore her honor or die trying." Mark frowned when he spied the coach bearing the Marquess de Gray's coat of arms, amid the small crowd that had gathered to observe the gentlemen's spectacle. How had he known his bride-to-be would not abide his request to forgo the duel? "Even if she is a tad willful."

"What woman is not? And I do not always approve of such contests, but I understand your position, and the blackguard certainly deserves it." Nelson dipped his chin, as a captain of the Royal Marines situated a table and then displayed a matched pair of flintlock pistols. "It appears your lobster has opted for firearms."

"Excellent." Clarendon arrived, looking rather pale, and Mark smirked. "Given the disparity in our physiques, swords would not have afforded a fair fight."

"Gentlemen, as per the rules for engagement set forth in the *Code Duello*, the party of the first offense may avoid the challenge and retain his honor by making a proper apology." The captain thrust his chest. "Second Lieutenant Clarendon, do you wish to make amends?"

"Most assuredly not." Clarendon sneered. "As I stand by my assertions."

"All right." The captain huffed a breath. "Let it be known that the party of the first offense waives the right to article one. In accordance with rule eighteen, I shall now ask the seconds to load and inspect the weapons."

"Oh, Mark." Just then, Amanda charged the fray and wrenched the lapels of his frock. "Please, do not do this. I beg you, as it is not necessary."

"Amanda, return to your coach, and cover your eyes." He wiped her tear-stained cheeks. "None of that, love. If you intend to marry a naval man, you must be brave."

"But you need not risk your life." Then she whispered, "We can sail away. We could move to Jamaica or even India."

"You would do that for me?" Despite her fear, she warmed his heart and strengthened his resolve. "You would abandon your home, your family, and your position in society, to be with me?"

"*Yes*." Her eyes flared. "Because I have nothing without you."

"Dearest Amanda, the damage to your reputation is a permanent stain on your family and their legacy." He cupped her chin. "Need I remind you that polite society is anything but polite, and the scandal would follow us and our children? We could never escape it, and that is not the future I envision for us, so we will deal with it, here and now, as must needs."

"Is there not some other way?" She sniffled and then clutched his forearms. "I demand you identify an alternative solution."

"Oh, you are my officious little thing." He chuckled and then straightened, as her father approached. "Marquess de Gray, I would be in your debt if you would remove your daughter from the premises."

"Lieutenant Douglas, I am already beholden, so we shall consider the debt discharged." The marquess grabbed his errant offspring, dragged her half the distance to the coach, but she evaded his grasp. "Amanda, come with me."

"Wait." Again she ran to Mark, pulled a folded handkerchief from her bodice, and kissed the linen square. "Wear this in your coat, over your heart. And tomorrow night, at the Chatham ball, I shall bestow upon your lips that which I placed on this humble scrap of cloth."

"Thank you, darling. And I shall hold you to your promise." He pressed the lace-edged lady's accouterment to his nose, inhaled her perfume, and then obeyed her command. "Now go with your father, and do not witness the events, so I may concentrate and prevail."

"As you wish." She opened her mouth and then closed it. "Mark, I—"

"Gentlemen, the seconds have dispatched their duty." The captain clicked his heels. "It is time."

"Amanda, leave the area—now." Mark glanced at Captain Nelson and said, "Are we ready, sir?"

"Aye." Nelson nodded once and handed over the pistol. "She is loaded."

"Thank you, sir." Mark checked his future wife and discovered her on the verge, tucked in her father's embrace, with her back to the scene. "Let us be done with it."

"If both parties will assume their respective positions." The army captain scrutinized Mark's stance. "Gentlemen, I shall count ten paces, upon the completion of which you shall turn, aim, and fire."

With a tight grip of the butt, Mark inhaled a deep breath and peered at the sky. Time suspended as an eerie calm invested his frame. Visions of his lady, warm and inviting in his bed, soothed his frazzled nerves, and then he cleared his mind.

"One...two...three...four...five...six—"

Gunfire rent the air, followed by a piercing feminine scream.

Given years of combat at sea, his initial instinct was to duck. After discerning he had suffered no injury, Mark glanced over his shoulder and spied Clarendon, with a sheepish expression and his arm outstretched, the smoking flintlock in his clutch.

"Second Lieutenant Clarendon, you are without honor." The captain drew his sword, as had Clarendon's support. "You will remain where you are, sir. First Lieutenant Douglas, as you were."

"But—he missed." In light of the coward's premature ejection, and subsequent public shaming, Mark considered the matter closed. "It is hardly an equitable challenge."

"Be that as it may, the rules are implicit and non-negotiable," explained the captain. "You must discharge your weapon, sir."

And so Mark shrugged and resumed his stance, and the captain recommenced the countdown.

"Seven...eight...nine...ten."

In an instant, Mark turned on his heel and leveled the barrel. Once again, to his unutterable frustration, his lady appeared at the perimeter of the action, and he rolled his eyes.

"Lady Amanda, hold hard." Damn willful woman. But then

he studied her countenance, as the marquess and Helen joined Amanda, and he noted the terror straining his stubborn debutante's delicate features, the rigid set of her shoulders, and the noticeable quiver of her chin, so he reconsidered his predicament. While he desired a measure of retribution, which he viewed as balm to his pride, he wanted Amanda more. Inclining his head, Mark aimed and then said, "Clarendon, if you value your life, make your apologies to Lady Amanda, and convince me of your sincerity and regret, else I will dispatch you to your maker."

"Oh, I say." Clarendon all but danced a jig, and then a telltale stain appeared at his crotch.

"You must be joking." Captain Nelson scoffed. "What a disgrace to the marines. Were you a sailor, I should have you docked at half-pay."

"Out with it." Mark bared his teeth. "*Now*."

"My agreeable Lady Amanda Gascoigne-Lake, please accept my most humble expression of remorse for the unkind words of yesterday afternoon." Clarendon winced, when Mark arched a brow. "I am truly sorry for any distress my inappropriate conduct caused. Know that I remain your unworthy servant."

"Lady Amanda, are you satisfied?" Mark kept the milksop in his sights.

"No, I most certainly am not." She thrust her adorable chin, which she now set firm, folded her arms, and humphed, and how he ached to kiss her silly. "I believe Second Lieutenant Clarendon insulted you, too."

"My lady is unhappy, Clarendon." Mark bit his tongue to keep from laughing. "You shall gratify her, or I will spill your blood. The choice is yours."

"Most noble First Lieutenant Douglas, I do apologize for my offense." Clarendon swallowed hard and appeared to teeter on the brink of an apoplectic fit, as he glanced at Amanda. "You are a credit to your uniform, sir. And I should endeavor to emulate your generous example."

"And *now* is Lady Amanda content?" Mark narrowed his stare.

For a few seconds, his officious little thing delayed, as she tapped a finger to her cheek and held Clarendon in suspense. When she cast Mark a flirty smile, he could not help but grin. At long last, she heaved a sigh. "Oh, I suppose if Lieutenant Douglas is appeased, then so am I."

In a flash, Mark redirected the pistol and fired into the ground—and Clarendon collapsed, unconscious, on the grass.

A throng of revelers swamped Mark, extending their congratulations for a job well done. And much to his surprise, a bevy of young beauties, including the two snobs from the night he met his lady, vied for his attention, but there was only one face he sought, which remained conspicuously absent. As the crowd dissected and relived the events, he located his society miss on the green, in the company of the marquess and Helen.

"Bloody good show, Douglas." Helen erupted in boisterous mirth. "Even though you shed no blood. You should have shot that namby-pamby in the arse."

The marquess extended his hand. "First Lieutenant Douglas—"

"Please, call me Mark." He accepted the customary male greeting, in friendship.

"And as you so gallantly defended my family's honor, you must address me informally, as Hiram." The marquess chucked Mark's shoulder. "You have made quite an impression on my wife and my daughter, so I should like to invite you to dinner, Saturday next, as it seems we have business to discuss."

"Thank you, for the magnanimous gesture, and I am obliged to accept." And he would secure his lady's hand in marriage.

"But in regard to the duel, I only did what polite decorum required."

"As usual, you are too modest, Lieutenant Douglas." Amanda stuck her tongue in her cheek. "Papa, cousin Helen, may I have a minute with my hero, in private?"

Her father frowned. "Amanda—"

"Papa, I can hardly be compromised in the middle of Paddington Green, with countless spectators present." His haughty miss folded her arms, and Mark vowed she would never bend him as she had her father. "You can guard me from our coach, as you can see me clearly from there."

"All right, but do not linger, or I shall collect you, and you will not enjoy it." The marquess elbowed Helen. "Come along, my dear. Let us allow my daughter a moment to congratulate her champion."

Summoning patience, Mark bade his time. She shuffled her feet and cleared her throat. He raked his fingers through his hair, and then he met his lady's gaze. Amusement danced in her blue eyes, and he sighed.

"You disobeyed my request to stay home." He rested hands on hips. "I ought to heat your posterior."

"My dashing Lieutenant Douglas, I will never be ruled by that which I do not do of my own free will, and if we are to build a family, I had better start out as I mean to go on. Anything less would be dishonest, and if you do not appreciate it, you may feel free to plant your affections elsewhere." And then her composure broke, and she shook her first. "But if you do—well, you just try it, and see what happens. And if you wish to punish me, I shall be delighted to present my bottom for your inspection."

Mark burst into laughter at her glorious display of temper. In a scarce second, he imagined his palm pressed to her delectable derrière, and his Jolly Roger stood at full salute. It was as though he had just returned home, from a lengthy voyage, and he could make love to her as fifty men. "Amanda, what am I to do with you?"

"Why, whatever you wish, sir." With an impish grin, she whispered, "I am at your disposal."

"That is an offer I dare not refuse." He spied the marquess, pacing before the coach. "But your father grows impatient, and you already owe me a boon, which I intend to collect, tomorrow night, at the Chatham's."

"Until then, my Mark. And thank you, for restoring my honor." Amanda stepped to the side but halted. "One more thing, if I may impose further on your hospitality."

"My Amanda, you are never an imposition." He sketched a proper bow. "What would you have of me?"

"Only this, which I impart with all my heart." Bold and unafraid, she stiffened upright and met his stare, and what he saw there quite stole his breath away. "I love you."

~

THE CAVERNOUS BALLROOM at the Chatham's London residence boasted a painted ceiling by Francis Hayman, in his signature French Rococo tradition, and sixteenth century Italian embroideries covered the walls. Despite the sheer magnitude of the space, the sparse combination of crystal chandeliers and candelabra, along with strategically placed bouquets of hothouse winter mixes, lent the venue a cozy, romantic aura, which made it a favorite event of the Little Season, for beaus and their ladies.

"Will you stop fidgeting?" Cousin Helen rolled her eyes. "Just watching you makes my big toe hurt. And you cannot possibly doubt that he will show, after he risked his neck to save your reputation."

"I know, but he failed to pay call this afternoon, neglected to escort me to the Promenade this evening, and I am at a loss to explain why." In silence, Amanda wondered if her ill-timed declaration had something to do with Mark's uncharacteristic and unappreciated absence. Had she frightened her heretofore-intrepid sailor? If that were the case, then it was a bit of good luck she had been interrupted prior to the gentlemen's contest, as she had intended to send her dashing lieutenant into battle shielded with her pledge of eternal devotion.

"And what have you done with your wardrobe?" Helen arched a brow. "Although your signature style is fashionable, of late your color palette consists of a singular shade, and dare I ask the reason?"

"Now you know I have always had a fondness for the hue." Amanda sniffed and assessed her velvet gown trimmed in old gold. "After all, my father is an admiral, and Mark favors me in navy blue."

"Daresay he would favor you *out* of navy blue, too." Helen waggled her brows and chortled. "As I have seen how he looks at you when he thinks you unaware."

"Oh?" Amanda pretended indifference, though she desperately wanted to believe her brash relation. "And how is that?"

"As a man just returned from lengthy maneuvers." She elbowed Amanda in the ribs. "And I would wager he would like to conduct extended maneuvers with you."

"*Helen.* Keep your voice down, as someone might hear you." Amanda scanned the immediate vicinity, tamped her expectations, which had flown the roof, and grabbed her cousin. "Do you really think he desires me, or do you say so for my benefit?"

The quirky spinster narrowed her stare. "Well—"

"Lady Amanda." John Markham, the Earl of Woverton, bowed. "Might I request the pleasure of the allemande, this evening?"

"Lord Woverton, you are too kind, and had I any openings on my dance card, I should accommodate you." Falsehoods were not her forte, so she braced for an impending lightning strike. "Alas, I must decline your gracious offer."

"How exceedingly cruel of you, Lady Amanda." He winked. "Perhaps, the next time."

"Of course, my lord." She counted to three and then cornered Helen. "Where is Mark? What has come of him? I cannot endure the suspense."

A commotion in the hall caught everyone's attention. Cheers and commendations reverberated off the walls, and then spontaneous applause erupted, as Mark strolled into the ballroom. Swamped by well-wishers, he disappeared amid the throng, including a bevy of beauties, even as Amanda leaped on her feet in an attempt to gain a view of her errant hero.

"What did I tell you? And stop hopping about like a rabbit." Helen clucked her tongue. "As it is, I would bet my monthly stipend he reports for your inspection, posthaste."

In that instant, Mark met Amanda's gaze, and she smiled; yet he remained stoic. For a few seconds, he stared at her, but she could glean nothing from his demeanor. Then he gave her his back, and her confidence sank to a new low.

Puzzled by his reticence, she searched her memory for a clue to his exasperating behavior. After his much-professed ardor in the park, he acted as though she were a stranger. And yet common sense reminded her that passion had not equated love.

As the quartet signaled the first waltz, she remained at sea among the spectators. Unwilling to quit the field without a single charge, she ventured to the smoking room and lingered in the opening. It was the men's domain, so her presence would garner sharp rebuke were she to cross the threshold. When she spied her lieutenant, she waved, yet he paid no heed. Dejected and rejected, she retraced her steps.

For the second selection of dances, Amanda hugged the side wall and sheltered in the shadows, as her erstwhile suitor had since removed to the card room, without so much as a by your leave. When Helen granted the quadrille to a distant relative, Amanda strolled to a large, floor to ceiling outset window. With a quick glance from left to right, she slipped behind the drapery.

Admiring the starry sky, she rested her head against the casement and wrapped her arms about herself, as vignettes of the life to which she had aspired played a fanciful accompaniment to the lilting notes of the music, which had done little to improve her mood. Nothing about the night had gone as she had planned. Worse, it appeared Lieutenant Douglas no longer considered her *his* Amanda. With something between a sob and a sigh, she surrendered to the pain.

"What are you hiding from, my Amanda?" Mark chuckled, turned her to face him, and winced. "Why are you crying, love?"

"Does it matter?" As he wiped her cheeks, she frowned. "And why do you care? I see you are popular, tonight. Certainly too busy for me."

"Amanda." When she tried to retreat, he held her firm. "Do not be angry with me, as we must be careful not to rouse suspicion. In light of the duel, everyone watches us."

"And that matters? You are all friendliness and easy manners, sir. Even as you ignore me." When she attempted to avoid his scrutiny, he cupped her chin and pinned her with his stare. "I suppose I should be magnanimous in the wake of your chivalry, so I shall make you the same bargain you once offered me, though I should be more beneficent. If you changed your mind, if you have any reservations, you should proclaim them, now. While I shall be a vast deal more than disappointed, I shall be kind, and I will not be angry with you. You have my word, as a lady, I would abide your preference."

"Bloody hell." Mark blinked, stammered, and sputtered. "Do you hear that? It is your favorite, darling. Waltz with me."

His reluctance to respond to her proclamation sounded a

death knell from her perspective, and she plummeted to impressive depths, even as he enfolded her in his embrace. Determined to force his hand, to make him admit his misgivings, she now met his gaze. As they whirled amid a crush of elegant debutantes and debonair dandies, the couples passed in a blur. A ripple of awareness, tiny, at first, swirled and soared, carrying them ever higher, cocooning them in soothing warmth.

Conscious of nothing save the beat of her heart and the man for whom she had set her cap, she yielded to the enticing sensations he provoked, even as he manifested the source of her discomfit.

"You tremble, sweet Amanda." Mark squeezed her fingers. "What have I done to upset you?"

What could she tell him? How could she form the words to convey the torment wreaking havoc with her insides? And if she could describe the length of her despair, could she even summon the strength to speak, given the agony clawing at her chest and welling in her throat? Helpless, she studied his countenance.

The dinner bell pealed, and Mark anchored her at his side.

"Well, now, how are the young—" Helen peered at Amanda and gasped. "Merciful heavens, what happened?" She glanced at Mark. "All right. Follow me, and I shall brook no refusals."

"Lead the way, fair Helen." Mark clicked his heels and laughed, but Amanda found no humor in their exchange.

Arm in arm, with her hesitant suitor, she entered the dining hall. When her cousin commandeered a table for two in a dimly lit corner, Amanda steeled herself for the onslaught that his proximity often kindled.

"What a perfect place to take your ease, as I shall sit near the buffet." Then, in an earsplitting tone, Helen said, "I require a seat to prop my foot—my big toe, you know. But I will be watching you, so no busy hands."

Mortified, Amanda uttered no complaint as Mark ushered her to a chair and then brought his beside hers. A cold chill of dread settled in her breast, as she pondered his reply. Why would he delay? What had he hoped to achieve? Had he feared she might enact a scene?

"Are you hungry, love?" Mark shifted his weight and bent his head. "Shall I fetch you a plate?"

Oh, why would he not confess his disinterest and have done with it?

"Amanda, please, this grows tedious." Then he snapped his fingers. "Ah, I know my lady's fondness. Do not run away, as I shall return, darling."

She found no joy in his term of endearment, as he had not expressed his penchant. Peering to the side, Amanda frowned at Helen, who shrugged, furrowed her brow, and then compressed her lips.

"And here we are for my lady, a Shrewsbury cake and a glass of champagne." Mark set the items on the table. "And I thought I would share your fancy, as I have secured my own portions. To what shall we toast?"

For a minute, she simply traced the damask pattern on the burgundy cloth. At last, it was too much to bear. In that instant, Amanda closed her eyes, and a tear coursed her cheek.

"Amanda, talk to me." Mark groaned, a weighty affectation she felt to her core. "What is wrong?"

"Why should I answer your query, when I await your, as yet, unstated preference?" She picked a speck of lint from her sleeve. "Admit it, you no longer want me."

"Look at me."

"No."

"Amanda, look at me."

At last, she obeyed.

"Oh, sweetheart." He cast a quick peek over his shoulder,

and then he clutched her hand and drew it beneath the table linens to rest on his thigh. "My darling girl, can you not see? Have I not warned you are temptation, personified? Do you not comprehend the extent of my torment? Of course, you are an innocent, so you cannot conceive of my anguish."

"Have I hurt you?" Confused, she recounted the past few weeks for some hint of reproach. "Did my declaration embarrass you? Is that why you did not visit me this afternoon or escort me in the park?"

"No. But I suspect I have hurt you, and I should sooner take my own life than cause you distress." He shook his head. "My well-intentioned but naïve seductress, you offer a kiss in payment for the restoration of your honor, yet I could never restrain myself to that treasure, and I would not exchange one stain upon your reputation for another, as you are too important to me. You struck a mortal wound from which there is no escape, and the balm is such that we cannot indulge until we are wed. But I assure you, when deprived of your company, and it is a trial I can scarcely endure, you are never far from my thoughts."

"Oh, Mark." Hope blossomed, and Amanda inhaled a shaky breath and twined her fingers in his. "I feel the same, as I ache for you."

After another surreptitious glance at Helen, he studied Amanda's lips, and she fidgeted beneath his examination, which left her giddy. But when he slipped his thumb inside her glove to caress her palm, skin to skin, she shivered, and he winked.

"At night, I dream of you, soft and feminine in my arms. In the light of day, I envision our future, and it has become a most cherished pastime altogether new to me." He leaned near and whispered, "I want to take care of you, yet you are my officious little thing, so you need me not. But I want to hold you when your belly is round with my child, to calm your fears when you are alarmed, and to comfort you when you are in pain. I would cry with you when you are sad, and laugh with you when you are happy. For you, alone, I would kill a thousand men, if only to be your champion. This I say, while leaving even more unsaid, if only to make you understand. My Amanda, I love you, too."

CHAPTER FOUR

"Do you feel better, fair Helen?" Mark caught the eccentric spinster, as she teetered. "Perhaps we should return to the ballroom, where you might take your ease."

And he needed to find his Amanda, after his ill timed, hastily composed oratory in the Chatham's dining room. Given the sheer force of his emotion-driven declaration, and her youth and inexperience, it would not surprise him to discover he had frightened her, and he had to explain his motives. Yet her inner torment had leveled his defenses, and he could not, in good conscience, allow her to labor under mistaken assumptions, when reality presented circumstances to the contrary.

"Will you keep your blasted voice down?" She steered him to the right, along a narrow path. When they encountered an illicit rendezvous, she choked with exaggerated volume. "Oh, my big toe, how it pains me."

"And do you know where Amanda has disappeared, as I must speak with her?" He ducked to avoid a decumbent branch, and then he scanned the immediate vicinity. His lady had said nothing after his fervent pledge, had only excused herself after dinner, and he languished in a white-capped ocean of indecision. "We stroll farther from the main house with each successive step. I may have to carry you back, if we do not retract our course."

The expansive gardens manifested myriad dark spaces for conducting naughty deeds, so it was a bit of good fortune that he had opted to forgo his appointment with Amanda, as he yearned to commit all manner of naughty deeds with her. The center yard boasted an eclectic mix of rose bushes, topiaries, vine-covered pergolas, and, in the distance, off to the side, a diminutive gazebo, which had been situated beneath the immense canopy of a massive oak. Filtered by the foliage, moonlight cast a silvery mosaic on the grounds. As they neared the petite structure, he narrowed his stare and focused on a figure looming in the shadows. Based on the height and proportions, of which he dreamed every night, he solved the mystery of his missing lady.

"Remind Amanda to re-enter the Chatham's via the side doors, where I shall await you in the library," Helen whispered. "And if you make her cry again, young Douglas, you will answer to me, and it will not be pleasant. Now, do not tarry, as we must return to the ballroom, together, before anyone discerns our game. So make haste."

As Helen scurried back toward the grand residence, Mark bent to avoid another low-lying bough. Shrouded in darkness, he stubbed the tip of his boot on an exposed root and tripped. A soft, feminine giggle confirmed his suspicions. Perched on the second step, which brought her within striking distance, given the disparity in their stature, his lady welcomed him with outstretched arms. With one last check of the surroundings, he peered over his shoulder, and then he turned—right into Amanda's kiss.

How many nights had he dreamed of that moment, of the singular fragment in time when benevolent fate smiled upon him, and he claimed the first taste of his Amanda's sumptuous lips, lush and ripe as a pomegranate? Too many to count. But even in his wildest imaginings, he had not conjured anything as decadent as the genuine article. And he wanted more.

With infinite care, he sampled the sensuous indulgence she rendered with unshakeable persistence. When he attempted to retreat, she framed his face with her delicate hands, all but refusing to relinquish the ground she had captured, and how she had captured him. So with nary a thought for propriety or prudence, he prodded her with his tongue and could have cried when she opened to him.

For several heated, desperate, achingly sweet minutes, he licked and suckled in a frisky contest, and his Amanda proved a fast learner, meeting his voluptuous tack with a luscious counterassault of her own. To his abiding delight and imponderable frustration, her characteristic derring-do infused every titillating, if unschooled, caress. And yet, despite her inexperience, she seduced him.

Pulse points blazed to life, muscles tensed, and every nerve charged. And to his utter mortification, his Jolly Roger seemed to possess an unusually exuberant mind, as it was overly jolly and only too ready to plow her uncharted harbor. But his Amanda was no dockside doxy, so he resolved to preserve her virtue, even if it killed him—and it might.

At last, he broke their kiss. Resting forehead to forehead, Mark marshaled his wits, even as Amanda shivered in his embrace and pressed her tantalizing curves to his stalwart frame. Before he toppled her to the floor of the garden structure, and seized her virginity then and there, he sought to distance himself from her siren song, but she held fast, clinging as a luxurious blanket.

"How dare you suggest I know not your torment, when I suffer every minute we are apart?" She nipped his chin. "At night, I dream of you, too. Often I wake in the early hours, to discover what I had thought real was nothing more than an illusion, and the subsequent emptiness and disappointment is almost more than I can bear."

"Darling Amanda." Despite a silent rebuke, he settled his palms to the twin swells of her bottom, anchored her, and pressed what had to be the most stubborn erection known to humanity to her belly. "You know not the danger you court."

"Yes, I do. And I am yours for the taking." She scored her fingernails to the nape of his neck. "Like you, I plan for our future, and I *long* to have your child. As you serve His Majesty, I would serve you. As you safeguard our shores, I would safeguard our home. With you at my side, whether in person or in spirit, I shall know no fear or pain. And while sadness and happiness are part of life, and I expect we shall know both, the former shall hold no sway, as the latter will persist if only I am your lady."

"You are my Amanda—never doubt that." He rubbed his nose to hers. "Even though I do not deserve you."

"Oh, yes, you do, my dashing Lieutenant." She trailed feathery kisses along his jawline, and he shuddered. "And I understand you would kill a thousand men for me, although I would never ask it of you, yet you need not resort to such drastic measures, as you are already my champion for having restored my honor without bloodshed."

"Well said, sweetheart." Her declaration worked on him in ways he could not have foreseen, and Mark concentrated on the simple repetitive act of inhaling and exhaling, to distract him from the overwhelming urge to claim her in the most elemental fashion. "And now that I have collected my boon, we should return to the ball and—"

"No, as I am not finished with you, sir." With an iron grip on the lapels of his coat, she yanked hard, gaining the full attention of every inch of him, and a few dangerous ones in particular.

"And never think that I need you not, as you are as vital to me as the air I breathe."

And with that, she emitted a half-strangled cry and came at him with force sufficient to knock him on his arse, had he locked knees, and he stumbled to keep them upright. Twining her fingers in his hair, his wanton society miss bit his lower lip and then besieged his mouth. In mere seconds, they erupted.

In an instant, an awkward test of will commenced, as his Amanda advanced with an intoxicating passion impossible to deny, and he retrenched in a last-ditch effort to maintain his sanity and her maidenhead. But, God, she was delicious.

Rational thought abandoned him, as he sailed on an alluring tide. Drawing on years of well-honed finesse in the sensual arts, he stroked and fondled her peaks and valleys, stoking the flames of desire, offering her no quarter. Operating on instinct, he nurtured and then fed an all too familiar hunger. And his lady made a valiant attempt to keep stride, with wild and hedonistic moves he found inexpressibly beguiling.

"Oh, Mark." Panting, she collapsed against him. "Is there not something we can do, as I burn for you?"

"Amanda, we cannot risk discovery." How captivating she was when heated with lust, and his heretofore-vaunted self-control fractured. "Even now—"

"Please?" She caught his earlobe between her teeth and hissed. "I beg you, do not leave me in this state, as I shall go mad for wanting you."

"Bloody hell." Never had he conceived that she might pine for him as he pined for her, with equal fervor. Before he could compose a protest, which might stay his curious debutante and the beast raging below his belly button, she thrust her hips, and he groaned. And First Lieutenant Mark Andrew Douglas, the notoriously disciplined second in command to Captain Nelson, was undone. "Do you trust me?"

"Yes," quick as a wink Amanda replied.

In a flash, he bent, swept her into his arms, and ascended the remaining stairs. The cozy, pentagon-shaped gazebo sheltered in the shadow of the oak's thick trunk and afforded the perfect hideaway for a clandestine tryst. With privacy chief among his concerns, he opted for the bench that faced the path, as he could spy any unfortunate interloper prior to discovery and conceal his future wife from prying eyes.

When the velvet-encased temptress squirmed in his lap, he sucked in a breath. "Amanda, sit still."

"I cannot." She wiggled and bucked. "It hurts."

"I know, darling." Cursing his carelessness, he stared at the ceiling and mentally plotted his tack with ruthless precision. In an effort to gain some semblance of control, he rolled his shoulders and gritted his teeth. With her needs as his principal priority, he untied the ribbon at her bodice, loosened the garment and the chemise, set his hand to her bare breast, and halted. Had she withdrawn in any measure, or expressed even the minutest amount of fear, he would have ceased his tender offensive. Amanda had not so much as flinched. "All right, love. There are ways to satisfy the hunger that ails you without the deflowering, but you must do as I say."

"Tell me, and I shall obey." She arched her back, and he doubted her oath. "*Please.*"

The provocative lady could not have known it, but she had just uttered the one word guaranteed to undermine his personal fortifications.

Claiming another boon, but mindful it was not one she had intended to share, he licked her pert nipple and paused for her response. She sighed, and he chuckled. Again and again, he suckled and laved her responsive flesh, pressing on her a gentle massage calculated to calm. As she relaxed in his embrace, with a rhythmic rush of whimpers playing an arresting accompaniment, he walked his fingers to the hem of her skirt, flicked up the heavy material, and located the lace trim of her garter. At a monotonous pace, he traced tiny circles along the sensitive inner side of her thigh, yet she sounded no alarm.

Following the pattern he had devised, he brushed the curls at the center of her core and waited for her reaction. For about a minute, he sensed she watched him in the dark, and then she cupped his cheek. Then, to his unutterable surprise, she spread her legs wide in unmistakable invitation.

Grateful for the dim conditions of their refuge, he fought uncharacteristic tears, as her implied surrender touched him beyond comprehension and fostered emotions he never knew he possessed. Lost in the moment, Mark covered her lips with his and thrust a finger inside the succulent folds at the apex of her thighs.

In concert with his thumb at the nub of her desire, he set an unhurried cadence in her honey harbor, as their tongues twined. Then, at regular intervals, he built speed, tapping a drumbeat in accordance with the maddening twist and turn of her hips and her muted moans.

All too soon, Amanda yanked and pulled his hair, just as her body went rigid with completion, but she remained true to her promise, with nary a shriek. Then and there, he promised himself he would have her screaming with pleasure on their wedding night. And then her magnificent contractions rippled about his finger, gathered steam, seared a path from his hand to his gut, and the loaded cannon in his crotch fired a violent volley in his breeches, which left him gasping in relief and astonishment.

How long Mark sat there, grinning like a fool, he neither knew nor cared—until he realized his lady wept. "Why are you crying, my Amanda? Did I hurt you?"

"No. Mine are happy tears, as you cannot hurt me, my love."

She shifted and nuzzled him. "It is just that I never knew it could be so beautiful."

"Neither did I, darling." He kissed her temple, as he withdrew his finger from her supple sheath and pulled down her skirt.

"Are you a virgin, too?" she asked in a small voice.

"What a curious question." And how the deuce should he answer her? Expecting—demanding honesty from his lady, he had to respond in kind. "No, Amanda. At six and twenty, I am no green lad."

"I see." She sounded deflated, and he hurled a slew of silent invective on his head for ruining an otherwise memorable occasion. Sitting upright in his lap, she resituated her bodice. "*Oh*? Then it was special for you, as well?"

"You truly are my officious little thing." With a hearty chuckle, he pondered the force of his climax and stretched his booted feet. "Dearest, you were superb."

"Thank you, my dashing Lieutenant." She giggled and slid from his embrace. "I suppose we should return to the ball, else Helen may search for us."

"Then let us away." Mark buttoned his coat to conceal the evidence of their assignation. "As she is not a woman I would cross."

"And neither am I, so I shall see you Saturday, for dinner at my home?" She accepted his proffered escort and rested her palm in the crook of his elbow. "You will attend, will you not?"

"Of course, as I am not daft." They strolled along the gravel path. "Whereupon I will ask your father for your hand in marriage and secure his permission to fix a date for our wedding."

∼

STANDING before the long mirror in her chamber, Amanda assessed the low-cut bodice of her blazing red velvet gown and smiled. Her lieutenant would never know what hit him. And then she closed her eyes and revisited their tryst in the Chatham's gazebo. What he had done with his hands and his mouth, and how he had made her feel. And, oh, what she felt. Without thought, she cupped her breast, rubbed the back of her neck, and shivered.

"Amanda, your Lieutenant Douglas has arrived." Amanda flinched, just as her mother appeared in the entrance from the sitting room. "And you should rescue your beau before your father scares him. Daresay he learned quite a bit of mischief when your sister married, and he seems determined to put that knowledge to use. Plus, Helen is here, and you know what happens when those two combine their efforts."

"Stuff and nonsense, Mama." Amanda turned to the side and checked her profile. "Mark fears nothing. But I am excited to see him, so let us join them."

Following in her mother's wake, Amanda inhaled a deep breath, as her dress grew more constrictive with each successive step that brought her closer to her man. Descending the grand staircase, she anticipated Mark's reaction when he spied her new finery, and delicious warmth simmered beneath her flesh. When she strolled into the drawing room, passion kindled the minute she met Mark's gaze. By the time he completed a thorough inspection of her attire, scrutinizing her from top to toe, she was breathless.

"Lady Amanda, you are a vision." Given they dined in residence, she opted to forgo gloves, so Mark brought her bare hand to his lips and ever so briefly touched his tongue to her knuckles.

"Good evening, Lieutenant." Her knees buckled, and he squeezed her fingers. "I am so pleased you accepted our humble

Loving Lieutenant Douglas

invitation. Shall we gather by the fireplace, as it is chilly tonight?"

"Amanda—"

"Papa, you cannot object to our minor relocation, as our family provides more than substantial chaperone." She ushered Mark to the hearth. "Do you think so little of Lieutenant Douglas that you expect he would compromise me in full view of my parents?"

"Oh, I say." Helen burst into laughter. "That is your daughter, Hiram."

"I blame you for her willful nature." Her father arched a brow and glared at her mother. "You encourage her without thought of the consequences."

As her progenitors argued the practicality and finer points of her upbringing, Amanda peered at Mark and grinned, which he mirrored to her absolute delight. "I have missed you."

"And I you, although I escorted you to the Promenade just this afternoon." He smirked. "Promise me something."

"Anything, my dashing Lieutenant." She radiated with excitement. "As I am at your service, unreservedly."

"I like the sound of that, and I would have your word, as a lady, that you will wear that gown on our honeymoon." After a surreptitious glance over his shoulder, he faced her. In a low voice, he said, "As I would peel that sumptuous garment from your body, inch by glorious inch."

"Oh, Mark." Amanda whispered, "I cannot stop thinking of the other night."

"Neither can I, sweetheart." He shifted his weight. "And I am quite relieved that our prurient pursuit has not shocked or alarmed you."

"Why should I be shocked or alarmed when I am with you?" She lifted her chin and steeled herself to pose the one question foremost on her mind. "As it stands, I have wondered if our meeting had given you pause for reflection, as it could not have been very satisfying for you."

"My naïve temptress, you have no idea how satisfying I found our liaison." Mark shuffled his feet and cleared his throat. "Suffice it to say, it benefitted me in equal measure."

"Really?" Puzzled, she pictured the moment in her mind. "But how can that be, as I did nothing to inspire you."

"Do not underestimate the power you wield over me, love." Mark chuckled. "Trust me, you did plenty."

She blinked. "I do not understand."

"You will once we are wed."

"Must we wait?" She bit her lip. "Can we not do it again? Next week is the final gala before the *ton* departs for their country estates to celebrate the holidays, so we have no time to lose."

"Are you not the naughty minx?" He clucked his tongue and narrowed his stare. "While nothing would give me greater joy, I would wait until we have made our vows."

"And I would have otherwise." She cast him a flirty pout. "Do you not want me?"

"You know very well I do, my Amanda." A red hue permeated his cheeks. "But I will not—"

"My lord, ladies, and gentlemen, dinner is served." The butler bowed.

"Thank goodness, as I am starved." Helen pressed a palm to her belly. "I am so hungry, I could eat my toenails."

"Including your much agitated big toe?" Mark inquired, as he escorted Amanda on his right and Helen on his left.

"Oh, do not remind me, young Douglas." Helen elbowed him in the ribs. "You know how my gout plagues me."

In the dining room, Mark pulled out a chair and settled Amanda, and she expected him to assume the seat beside her. To her dismay, he escorted Helen to the position at Papa's left, and then Mark perched on the opposite side of the table from Amanda. It was then she noticed the place settings. Of course, her parents would never allow her such proximity to her prospective husband, even in relaxed company.

The meal consisted of Papa's favorites, white soup, followed by a ragout of beef with a compliment of macaroni and cheese. It was simple but comforting fare, which Amanda needed at that moment, because her sire commenced the interrogation.

"So your father is Viscount Trematon?" Papa queried.

"Yes, sir." Mark nodded.

"And you are the second son." It was a statement, not a question.

"Indeed, sir." Mark glanced at her and winked. "But I am my own person."

"As I made you free with my name, you must call me Hiram." Her father signaled for another glass of wine. "How did you amass your fortune?"

"I saved my portion of the prizes taken at sea," Mark explained. "Some monies I invested in timber and tobacco, in the Americas, and I have enjoyed a substantial return. Also, I own a sugar plantation in Jamaica, but my workers are employed, as I will not support the practice of slavery. And my portfolio includes various properties in London, along with an estate in Kent."

"You have done well for yourself, Lieutenant." Her mother reclined in her chair, and Amanda knew Mark had snared Mama. "And very impressive at such a tender age."

"Please, call me Mark." How could he remain so calm, when Amanda wanted to scream, if only to ease the tension investing her frame? "And I learned the value of a pound as a boy, when the viscountcy fell on hard times."

How unfair was it that, as Mark charmed her parents, she found herself falling in love with him, all over again? And she ached for him, as he described his relationship with his older brother, who, despite the luck of birth, still viewed Mark as competition, much to her lieutenant's expressed regret and inability to resolve the conflict.

"And what are your plans for the future?" her father inquired.

"No offense, Hiram, but I want your job." Mark tugged at his crisp white stock.

"You aspire to the Admiralty?" Her father appeared surprised. "You are a career naval man?"

"I am, sir." The firm set of Mark's jaw underscored his tenacity. "There is no nobler profession, in my humble estimation, and I shall serve my commission until I die."

"Well said, Mark." How proud Amanda was of her sailor, and she yearned to kiss him.

"But, for some men, the sea is sufficient mistress," her mother added, with a frown. "To the detriment of all else."

In that instant, Amanda made a mental note to apologize to her sister. As her brother-in-law Henry had endured similar cross-examination, Amanda had teased and taunted Olivia, without mercy. Given her fragile nerves and unstable belly, Amanda feared she might embarrass herself, and it was no less than she deserved.

"That may be—for some men." Mark caught Amanda in a penetrant stare. "But my heart has plenty of room for a wife and children, with which God may see fit to bless us."

And so her beau anchored her, and she exhaled in relief.

"That is comforting to know, Lieutenant. And as we are family tonight, why do we not adjourn to the drawing room for our dessert and tea?" Her mother stood. "And I shall have the brandy brought from your study, Hiram."

"I need to speak with young Douglas, Eleanor." Her father

rubbed the small of his back, after he rose from his chair. "In private."

"It can wait until we have sampled your most cherished treat." Her mother smiled, and Amanda realized the entire meal had been planned to soften her father's mood for the impending discussion. "Cook made the apple snow just for you, and you would not want to disappoint her."

"All right, Eleanor." Her father chuckled. "You know, very well, apple snow always reminds me of my days in shortcoats."

And so they retraced their earlier steps, and Amanda led Mark to the *chaise*, near the hearth. As it accommodated only two, they could converse freely, if they lowered their voices.

"This looks delicious." Mark dug a healthy portion with his spoon.

"It is quite good, only I am not fond of the garnish." Amanda wrinkled her nose. "Would you like my cherry?"

"Given it is yours, it is all the more sweet." Mark waggled his brows. "So how am I doing?"

"Oh, Mark. You are indomitable, as ever." Amanda cast a surreptitious glance at her father. "I do not foresee any impediments to our nuptials. I mean, what objection could Papa have, in light of your excellent credentials, connections, and fortune?"

"*Indomitable*?" He snickered and blushed, and she craved his kiss. "High praise, sweetheart."

"Oh, quite indomitable, sir." She studied his lips and imagined them pressed to a wide variety of places on her body. "And I wish to marry soon."

"Define *soon*." He scraped clean his dessert dish. "As I can be summoned to Greenwich without notice."

"Then by Christmas, at least, and not a day beyond." She bounced with nervous excitement. "We would celebrate our first holiday, as husband and wife, and how I love the sound of that."

"All right, my officious little thing." He gave her a playful nudge. "We shall wed—"

"Douglas, it is past due for our discussion." Her father delivered his empty dessert dish to the tea trolley. "My study—now."

And just like that, the spell broke, and Amanda thought she might be physically ill.

"Wish me luck." Mark trailed the pad of his thumb along the curve of her cheek.

"You will not need it." She could only pray she was right. "But good luck, just the same." Alone, Amanda moved to sit beside her mother on the sofa.

"Oh, do not worry, my dear." Her mother offered a cup of tea, which Amanda declined with a shake of her head. "Your young man seems a strong, sensible sort."

"And he is in love with you." Helen snorted. "Daresay wedding bells shall ring before the New Year."

"Bite your tongue, Helen." Her mother scoffed. "How could I possibly plan a suitable ceremony in a mere fortnight?"

"Then perhaps you should begin preparations, posthaste, Mama." Amanda wrung her fingers. "Because Mark and I wish to take our vows, at once. And I expect he will ask Papa to secure a special license."

"Well you might have given me some warning, my dear." Her mother deposited her cup and saucer on the trolley and checked off an imaginary list. "First thing in the morning, I must contact the modiste, the milliner, and, oh bother, the archbishop. We must publish the banns, and I should speak with Cook about the menu for the reception."

At that very second, Mark stormed into the foyer. Amanda leaped from her seat, with Mama and Helen in her wake. When her father shook Mark's hand, Amanda squealed in delight. But then Mark clicked his heels and saluted.

"You may depend on me, sir. I will not fail you." And then

Mark, with a furrowed brow and a troubled gaze, faced her. "I am so sorry, Amanda."

With that, he turned and exited, without so much as a backward glance.

"Hiram, what has happened?" Her mother hugged Helen, as the two manifested palpable shock.

"Mark, come back." As her world teetered on end, Amanda made to follow, but her father caught her by the arm. With a plaintive cry, she wrenched free. "Papa, what have you done?"

CHAPTER FIVE

In the dark, Mark pulled the lapels of his coat and shivered, as the cold night air penetrated his uniform, and he remained in a state of heightened awareness. Given the dim light of the crescent moon, it would be just his luck to fall victim to some overzealous watchman. Glancing from side to side, he crept along the alleyway, which opened to the mews and the back gate described in the urgent missive Amanda had sent. For a few seconds, he loomed in the shadows, as he considered and reconsidered his exacting obeisance of her summons.

"*Psst.* Mark, are you there?"

"Amanda?" He nearly jumped out of his skin. "Is that you?"

"Hurry." The latch and hinges creaked in protest, as she swung open the tiny portal. "Before someone sees you."

"All right." He noted the expansive gardens and frowned. "Just what are you—"

"Will you be quiet?" She grabbed him by the wrist. "Come with me, and keep your voice down."

In silence, they wound their way along a narrow path, which twisted and turned through various flowerbeds, hedgerows, and a small maze, and then veered left, toward the main house.

They entered the elegant residence through the terrace doors, and Mark caught his toe on a piece of furniture. He winced, and Amanda halted, which caused him to bump into her.

"Shh." Then his lady brought his hands to rest on her waist, and the old Jolly Roger roused to full alert. "Stay close, as I could navigate my home with my eyes closed."

Once again, without serious reflection, Mark yielded to her request, despite thoughts to the contrary. From what he could gather, they entered a hallway and turned right. After a series of cautious maneuvers, she paused.

"There is a staircase here," she said in a whisper, ascended a single pace, and halted. "There are twelve steps, total, divided by a landing. You can count them."

"Amanda—"

"Hush." She giggled softly. "We will get where we are going, soon enough, and you may ask all the questions you wish, at our final destination, as we have much to discuss."

Ah, so that was her game. No doubt she had numerous inquiries regarding her father's refusal to allow their wedding, at least, not yet. But he had promised not to divulge the requisite conditions for their betrothal, so he would choose his words with care—and then he tripped. Jolted to reality, in his mind he muttered a caustic curse and then ticked off each successive footfall, as a guide.

At the second floor, Amanda marched straight ahead, as if going into battle, and Mark smiled to himself—until the marquess loomed as a specter of doom at the other end of the long hallway, illuminated by a single candlestick. In a flash, his lady sidled into a diminutive alcove, which lacked sufficient depth to shield them, should her sire rotate a mere quarter-turn. But the admiral opened a door and argued, presumably, with Amanda's mother.

As her parents quarreled, Amanda rested against Mark,

dropped her arms to her sides, and squeezed his thighs, which scored a direct hit to his loins, and he clenched his jaw. When she shifted, gazed at him, and mouthed, *I love you*; he mimicked her oath, bent his head, kissed her, and then hugged her tight.

"Eleanor, that is my final decision." The marquess stomped across the hall, slammed shut the oak panel, and darkness fell on the passage.

Amanda flinched, and then she resumed her course. It was then he discovered they were just shy of her targeted destination, as she opened the very next door and slipped inside, and he trailed her.

A fire burned in the hearth of the sumptuously appointed sitting room, which boasted telltale accouterments that declared it a woman's domain. Beyond a second entrance towered an impressive four-poster, with the linens turned down in unmistakable invitation, and Mark froze.

"Amanda, where have you brought me and to what purpose?" Even as he posed the query, he knew the answer. "This is not a good idea."

"I beg to differ, my dashing Lieutenant, as this is a most excellent idea and a noble purpose." She lingered in his wake. "And what have you to fear, as it is just you, I, and a comfortable bed."

"Trust me, that is the most dangerous combination known to humanity." Unable to tear his interest from the heretofore-innocuous piece of furniture, he swallowed hard. Aware of nothing save a desire to be gone from what he surmised was her private chamber he turned on a heel and discerned she had doffed her coat and slippers. "What in bloody hell are you wearing?" He averted his stare, even as his capriciously loaded cannon primed for a carnal crusade. "Or not wearing?"

"For a not-so-green lad, are you truly so unacquainted with

my attire?" She neared. "To be honest, I had it commissioned in anticipation of our nuptials, and I had hoped to please you. Are you not pleased?"

"Amanda, it is unwise to tempt a man, thus." Mark focused on the ceiling and rallied dispassionate thoughts, including images of Helen's gout-plagued big toe, which afforded serviceable results—until his lady wrapped her arms about his waist and pressed her silk-encased body to his. "Given that I cast off with the *Boreas* on tomorrow evening's tide."

"What?" Framing his face, she forced him to look at her. "When did you receive your orders?"

"Only today." He grimaced, as he had planned to spare her that detail in a letter he had yet to compose. "From your father."

"Oh, Mark." Tears welled, and her chin quivered. "Then we have no time to lose, as I shall be your lady, in deed, if not in name."

The significance of her words struck him as the icy waters of the Baltic. "No, Amanda. We cannot possibly—"

"Yes, we can, and we shall." Without hesitance, she trod into the bedchamber, and the cleft of her bottom, visible through the gossamer material, foundered his well-established probity and in its place provoked insatiable lust. "And the night grows old, so we must hurry."

"You cannot be serious." He followed at a safe distance, as he was disciplined, not dead, and her sheer nightgown manifested more an afterthought than a functional garment. "And you are my lady, so I would not treat you as a doxy."

"But I am quite serious, and I will be your wife, so this is nothing more than premature, but nonetheless remarkable, consummation of our union." And then she acted completely out of character for a gently reared virgin, when she whisked the diaphanous garb over her head, revealing an inexpressible fantasy of which he could not have conceived. "You will make me yours, now—tonight."

"Darling, you are not yourself." On tenterhooks, and clinging to the last vestiges of self-control, Mark comprised numerous arguments in opposition to her stance, none of which he suspected he possessed sufficient strength to deliver with any degree of conviction. "Amanda, your father—"

"—Can go to the devil." With that, she drew the pins from her black hair, and her lustrous locks cascaded over her creamy shoulders, in a stunning display no man enjoyed with his prospective bride until after the vows were sanctioned. With arms outstretched, and blue eyes blazing, she flicked her fingers. "Make me yours, irrevocably."

Myriad justifications swirled in his brain as a miasma of confusion. A sense of honor warred with hunger, duty with desire, and fortitude with fervency. In each instance, the latter won. And although he remained rooted to the spot, his debutante persisted without shame, in glorious spirit and courage no man, sane or otherwise, could resist.

Amanda had just crossed their Rubicon, and he poised on the banks.

In a flash, Mark retrieved an item from his pocket, and shrugged from his coat, which he flung to a small sofa. In minutes, he sent his stock and waistcoat to join the frock, and then he unfastened the hook at the throat of his lawn shirt. With two stern tugs, he discarded his boots. In a few strides, he stood toe to toe with her, and then he dropped to a knee.

"My Amanda, you offer me your most precious gift, and I am inclined to accept, in light of our difficult circumstances." And then the significance of his declaration weighed heavy on his heart, as his consent would bind them forever. "But I do so only if you respond, in kind, with my humble present, which I had created as a modest affirmation of our engagement. If you would take this token—"

"Yes, I accept." She held out her left hand, and he slid the unpretentious band of white gold on her third finger. "Oh, Mark. It is beautiful, and the engraving is masterful craftsmanship. *Ego dilecto meo et dilectus meus mihi.*"

"I am my beloved's, and my beloved is mine." He pressed his lips to her knuckles. "It is a poesy ring, meant to symbolize the depth and permanence of our commitment."

"How very Shakespearean of you, my romantic Lieutenant." And then with neither prompt nor encouragement, she pounced, knocking him on his back and showering his face in kisses.

Gathering his wits, it dawned on Mark that his Amanda, naked as the day she was born, sprawled atop him. In a scarce second, he reversed their respective positions, and he gave her his weight, as he rested a leg between her thighs. Thrusting his tongue in time with his hips, he hinted at the physical act she sought, as she squirmed and moaned beneath him.

"Amanda, are you sure about this, because once I claim you, there is no escape." They rested forehead to forehead. Despite his final warning, which he promised to abide, everything inside him signaled to charge her exquisite field. "You must marry me."

"My indomitable Lieutenant—"

"There is that word, again."

"Adequate to my man. And if you do not take me, I shall scream. Wait." Then she snapped her fingers. "What a wonderful idea. If Papa finds you here, he will force us to marry, and our problem is solved."

"Amanda—*no*." To his unmitigated horror, she opened her mouth, and he stifled her shout of alarm with his palm. "Are you out of your mind?" He glanced at the door, as if expecting her father to break through without notice. "The Admiral will kill me—*if* I am lucky, given my state of undress and your utter lack thereof."

With a countenance of amusement and a flirtatious giggle, which belied her objective, she unhooked his shirt. And then she wrested free and proclaimed, "I shall make you a bargain, my errant seducer. I will remain silent, if you give me something to occupy my time."

"All right. As my lady wishes." He groaned when she splayed her fingers across his bare chest. After a quick estimation of their locale, he refused to breach her on the floor, so he stood and swept her into his arms. As Mark lingered at the footboard of the four-poster, Amanda scored her nails to the nape of his neck and nipped his ear lobe, which struck a mortal blow to his defenses. "I loathe hurting you, any more than necessary, so we should avoid the bed for now."

"But—why?" The alacrity, the unmasked enthusiasm with which she submitted, evinced she had abandoned every effete precept she had been taught. "Is that not the usual place?"

With her singular goal in mind, he returned to the sitting room. Rotating, full circle, he inventoried the furniture at his disposal. To his chagrin, every scrap of hitherto utilitarian appurtenances presented enticing scenarios, which stretched the limits of his imagination, control, and breeches, but he filed them for future reference.

"Bloody hell." Fighting a wicked erection on which he could bounce guineas, given its rock-solid rigidity, until the New Year, he retraced his steps to her inner chamber.

"And now that you have made the grand tour of my apartments, shall we commence the deflowering?" Amanda nuzzled his temple. "Mark, just what are you about?"

"Hold hard, darling." Drowning in adventitious and

Loving Lieutenant Douglas

annoying nervousness, he huffed a breath in frustration. At a loss, he paused and contemplated the differences in their size, in relation to various coital positions, none of which inspired confidence when claiming a delicate virgin. At last, he settled on a large, overstuffed armchair, situated in a corner, near a window.

"What is wrong? Is my brave sailor intimidated by a little woman?" She licked the crest of his ear. "I promise, I will be gentle with you."

"Are we not comical?" After setting Amanda on her feet, he stripped off his shirt and then stuck his thumbs in his waistband. Just then, he glanced at his lady and discovered her stare fixed on his crotch, even as she bit her lip. "Sweetheart, have you revised your thinking?"

"No." She curled her toes. "My sister Olivia described her connubial experiences, upon return from her honeymoon, and that is the part of your anatomy that most fascinates me."

"Hell and the Reaper." At such frank honesty, Mark could not help but laugh. But despite her bravado, he spied trepidation in her visage and opted not to remove the pantaloons, as he would benefit from their restriction. Sitting in the chair, he slapped his thighs. "Come here, love."

"Like this?" she asked, as she straddled him.

"Perfect." Why was he not surprised that she complied without a moment's hesitation? He cupped her bottom. "Now scoot forward."

"You know, I really thought I might be—*oh*." Her gaze grew wide with wonder as the juncture of her supple core met the stout swell of his one-eyed pirate.

"You were saying?" His smug confidence faltered when she wiggled and fidgeted in his lap, and even through his breeches, she tantalized him beyond reason. But when she retreated to unfasten the hooks at his waistband, he grabbed her wrists. "Amanda, slow down."

"No, as I am determined, sir." And then her questing fingers found his erection, and he gritted his teeth. In mere seconds, the age-old question blossomed in her expression. "Mark, this cannot possibly work."

"It will, my officious little thing." Reclining, he sighed and tried to formulate a stern reproach about propriety and self-preservation, as she had no real inkling of how much he could injure her, how the initial intimate invasion could chill future relations, how his unchecked passion could consume her. In her innocence, in her vulnerability, she had not the strength to manage him, yet her blind trust left him reeling. Swimming against an alluring tide, he fought to regain his tack. Instead, he schooled her in the ways to stimulate a man, showed her where to stroke and fondle, and she took to his lessons with her customary relish. It was spectacular, having her pleasure him, and he gave himself into her unsophisticated but oh-so-sweet hands and floated on an illusory cloud of unfettered bliss. "*Yes.*"

But what his lady had done next well nigh slew him.

Bereft of reticence or apprehension, and with a directness that conquered his heart all over again, she shimmied and brought his length to her opening. Lost in his heaven on earth, he had not divined her aim until it was too late. Before he could halt her advance, she tilted her hips. On her second attempt, he lurched in a valiant but futile effort to deflect her, and he sailed right into her harbor, tearing through her maidenhead, and she flexed her thighs, holding his flesh deep within hers. Braced for her scream, he could have cried when she whimpered, leaned forward, and buried her face in the curve of his neck.

Inside him, something shattered.

"My Amanda, you disarm me." With infinite patience, he massaged her shoulders, the nodes of her spine, the small of her back, and then he simply held her, waiting for the eventual slackening of her muscles. "Relax, love. The pain will pass."

Of course, he had chosen their orientation to minimize her discomfit, while maximizing his direction of events, but his stubborn society miss had ideas of her own, as evidenced by her masterful and enchanting self-immolation. And he could not argue her goal, given the results, because, although she had not moved in a couple of minutes, he was near to exploding.

"So, that is it?" She shifted, he hissed, and she exhaled. With a brilliant smile, she rubbed her nose to his. "I am yours?"

"Indeed, you are mine. And this is only the beginning, love." And then he lifted her, stood, and carried his lady to the bed, whereupon he deposited her to the mattress, doffed his breeches, and covered her. In an instant, he joined their bodies. After instructing her how to wrap her legs about him, Mark cradled her head and kissed her. "Forever, Amanda."

And together they danced in a rhythm as old as time.

∽

Stretching long, Amanda yawned and winced at the soreness between her legs. As triumphant memories of the previous breathtaking night flashed in her brain, she smiled, moaned, and snuggled beside her naughty lieutenant. After their first fiery coupling amid the sheets, whereupon she had smothered her scream of exaltation with her pillow, Mark had roused her four more times during various hours and made sweet, gentle but passionate love to her.

"Mark Douglas, I shall love you till I die." She swept a lock of hair from his forehead, and he opened his eyes. "Did I wake you?"

"No." He shifted and pulled her close. "And my Amanda, I shall love you just the same. How do you feel?"

"Famished." She giggled. "As I have never worked so hard for my morning meal."

Just then, a knock at the door brought them both alert and upright.

"Breakfast is served in your sitting room, Lady Amanda," her maid called.

"Thank you, Ellie," Amanda responded, as she clutched the covers to her chin. "I shall ring for you when I am ready to bathe and dress."

"I set the bolt, after your ardent approbation of my nocturnal maneuvers, in the event your father discovered us," he whispered. "At the very least, it would have slowed him enough to give me a running start."

"Only if you can outpace a lead shot." Amanda envisioned the last and snorted, but her genial humor was short-lived. "Oh, no. If the servants are about, then so is Papa."

"Bloody hell." Mark leaped from the four-poster. "I thought you said you rose before the sun."

"On normal occasions, I do, but there is nothing normal about the dawn of this day, as I have scarcely slept a wink." After locating her nightgown, she pulled the silk over her head and then searched for a serviceable robe. "Because I was set upon in my bed by a marauding barbarian."

"Indeed you were, sweetheart." Fastening his shirt, he waggled his brows, and then he tugged on his boots. "And he quite enjoyed himself."

"Did you?" How she despised the nagging doubt plaguing their special moment. "I did not disappoint you, given your vast experience? And you will not dally with some exotic foreign woman, will you? While you are docked in a tropical port, somewhere far from me?"

"Amanda, how can you ask that?" He buttoned his waistcoat, walked to her, and drew her into his arms. "Foreign women are foreign women. You are exotic—and intoxicating, and enchanting, and irresistible, and I shall go mad for wanting you, until I see you again."

"Oh, Mark." Tears beckoned, and she squeezed him. "Must you go away?"

"None of that, now." He cupped her chin. "This is our life, the ever-changing world of the sea, should you choose to make our vows official and binding. How can I concentrate on my mission, if I am worried about you?"

"Last night bound us for eternity, and I thought Nelson's men did their duty." She swallowed hard. "So I should not signify."

"My dear, you are the exception to the rule." At the basin, Mark poured some water and washed his face. "And I would have you take care, as I will need you strong upon my return, because I shall make love to you as fifty men."

"I would settle for one man, Lieutenant." She handed him a towel and then fetched his coat. A familiar handkerchief fell to the floor, which she bent and retrieved. "You kept it?"

"Of course." As he donned his frock, she dabbed her perfume to the lace-edged linen square, before tucking it into his breast pocket. "I keep it next to my heart, per your command."

"That reminds me." She snapped her fingers, opened her armoire, and collected a small parcel. "This is for you. I had it commissioned as a wedding present."

"Thank you, darling." Clutching her hand, he pressed his lips to the poesy ring he had given her, and then he opened the box. "Amanda, it is beautiful, but it pales in comparison to you."

"It is a Cosway." The portrait miniature created by the appointed Painter to the Prince of Wales boasted an oval gold encasement encrusted with pearls and sapphires, the latter she chose to compliment her eyes. "Wear it, as a talisman against harm, so that you may come home, safe and sound, hale and hearty."

"As you wish." He tucked the memento into his coat. "I shall situate your image to my breast, as my personal guard. And now, much to my regret, I must away, as I am due in Greenwich. So how do you propose to free me from your lair of delicious iniquity?"

"Well, my original plan had been to sneak you down the back stairs, yet the staff has arisen." Tapping a finger to her cheek, she considered the possibilities. "Perhaps we should try, and I shall act as scout."

"All right." Mark bowed. "After you, my lady."

After unlocking the bolt, Amanda peeked into her sitting room. She waved at Mark, and they rushed to the door. Then she peered into the hallway and discovered it empty. Tiptoeing, she led him to the rear of the residence—but halted when her mother summoned a servant. Her lieutenant slammed into her but managed to keep them upright.

"Hurry," Amanda murmured *sotto voce* and waved. "The other direction."

They retraced their steps—and then her father, his nose in a periodical, appeared at the opposite end. Amanda skidded to a stop. She ventured left, Mark veered right, and they connected rudely in the middle. With his arms at her waist, he lifted her feet from the floor and ducked into nearby vacant guest quarters. For several minutes, he held her close, and then he bent his head and kissed her—and kept kissing her. When silence fell in their midst, they came up for air.

"What now?" Mark arched a brow.

"Of course." An epiphany quelled her unrest, and Amanda bit her lip. "Back to my room."

With a quick glance from side to side, they discerned the passage had cleared and ran to her chambers. Once again secure in her apartments, Amanda marched to the large window overlooking the east lawn. In haste, she twisted the lock and flung open the sash.

"Perfect." She assessed the predicament. "The trellis should hold you, and you can exit the gardens via the side gate, with none the wiser."

"It is only one floor, so I should survive if I fall." Mark made to throw his leg over the ledge but paused and pulled her into his embrace. Resting forehead to forehead, he said, "You have no idea how difficult it is to leave you."

"You have no idea how difficult it is to let you go." She caressed his cheek, even as her heart ached, and she dreaded their separation. "I miss you, already. And you will write me?"

"And I you." With that, Mark claimed one more soul-stealing kiss, which ended far too soon for her liking. "That shall have to sustain me through the voyage. And of course I shall write, and I ask the same of you, but I would caution you to remember the post is unreliable, at best, at sea. Correspondence is often transferred from ship to ship, before it is brought ashore, unless we put to port, so there may be delays."

After releasing her, he turned and shimmied out the window. Perched at the ledge, she monitored his progress, her agony increasing with each successive step that brought them further apart. Descending with care, he slipped when a rung broke beneath his weight, and she shrieked in horror. And then he resumed his downward climb, until he reached the bottom.

At his destination, he tipped his head and looked at her. "I love you, Amanda. Never forget that."

With a half-strangled cry, she fought the fast encroaching tears. "And I love you. Know that when next you dock in London, whenever that might be, I will be waiting for you."

For a long while, he simply stared at her, as if committing to memory the moment. The air sizzled with passion, forming an intimate connection that defied the distance between them, suffusing her with soothing warmth. Then, with his gaze locked on hers, he drew her handkerchief from his coat pocket and pressed it to his nose. Crestfallen, devastated by the cruel situation that had forced them to resort to such mischief, Amanda blew him a kiss and mouthed his name.

And then Mark was gone.

CHAPTER SIX

December yielded to January with a blustery gale, and Mark celebrated the New Year aboard the *Boreas*, as she patrolled the trade routes of the North Atlantic. More than a month had passed since he bade farewell to his lady, and yet he dispatched letters whenever they put to port to replenish stores. To his infinite disappointment, he had received nothing from his Amanda, despite her promise to write him.

Standing by the starboard rail of the quarterdeck, with the westerlies rustling his hair, he inhaled the familiar and comforting scent of brine mixed with kelp and dared not hope as they anchored alongside a Packet Service ship from Falmouth, bearing the King's flag, and official, as well as personal, correspondence was transferred between vessels. Regardless of his attempts to the contrary, he uttered a silent prayer that the canvas bags contained something—anything, for him.

Distraction, but no joy, was found in his examination of the polished boards, the grain of which shone bright in the sun, the falls flemished to his exacting specifications, and the devil had been fresh-paid with pitch at their last port. At the waist, the crew carried out their chores, whistling or singing naughty shanties as they worked. "Kennedy, secure the dry stores in the hold, with the swine."

"Aye, sir." The sailor saluted.

The second lieutenant emptied the first bag, and Mark sighed as despondency seeped into his muscles. Never had he relished the mail call, because his family had not written during his tenure at sea. And it was not for lack of caring but, rather, indicative of the characteristic Douglas stiff-upper-lip persona and their expectations to that effect. What he had come to realize since that first fateful meeting in the Northcote's ballroom was that Lady Amanda Gascoigne-Lake had changed his world and altered his view.

Yes, the mere wisp of a girl had penetrated his thoughts and, it seemed, every fiber of his being. While the navy life had always inspired his soul, it now all but consumed him, given the marquess's directive. The ocean appeared more nebulous, the canvas more crisp, and the sky more blue. Unfortunately, her absence had also impacted him, with quite the opposite results, and he genuinely ached for want of his Amanda. For the first journey since his days as a young, randy midshipman, he had put four fingers and a thumb to most excellent use.

"You are a fastidious lieutenant, Mr. Douglas." Captain Nelson scrutinized the gleaming deck, which bore not a speck of dust, from stem to stern, as the legendary naval man was correct in his assertion, and Mark would brook no less than perfection. "You lead by example, which is the best form of management, in my humble estimation, and have held your rank for these eight years, to your credit, so it is time for you to make post."

"I could not agree more, sir." Mark recalled the conversation in Admiral Gascoigne-Lake's study. "And the situation is more pressing than you can imagine."

The second lieutenant emptied another bag, and Mark shuffled his feet as ruthless dispiritedness traipsed his spine.

"So the rumors are true?" Nelson scanned the horizon with the bring-em-closer. "Old Hiram holds you to the same standard set by his father-in-law?"

"What?" He checked his tone. "I beg your pardon, Captain. Are you telling me—"

"That Lord Denning set identical requirements, when Hiram negotiated his engagement to Lady Eleanor." Nelson chuckled, closed the spyglass, and cast Mark an expression of sympathy. "Do not all proud papas want a naval captain for their daughters?"

"So it would seem." Mark frowned at the unfairness of it. "Yet there are no exams for which I can study to ensure success."

"No, there are none. Your fate is in your hands, as you must distinguish yourself to promote." Nelson grimaced. "And even then, you must agitate the Admiralty for a command, as I did after San Juan."

"*Douglas.*"

Mark snapped to attention. "Here."

The second lieutenant passed a sheaf of envelopes tied with twine, and Mark held his breath in anticipation. The minute he grabbed the bundle, he counted five letters, and his chest swelled, as his heart glowed, quelling the dank uneasiness that had plagued his frame for the past sennight, because he recognized the delicate script the minute he read his name on the top missive.

"*Billets-doux*, I daresay." Captain Nelson chortled and peered a-larboard. "And it seems they could not have come at a more opportune moment, as you blush, Mr. Douglas."

"I may be a tad under the weather, sir." Mortified that his superior had just put his finger on Mark's Achilles' heel, he tucked the dispatch in his coat pocket and cleared his throat.

"The effects of the cold, you know. And I took Eccleston's watch for the past three nights."

"If that is your story, Douglas, you stay with it." With a snort of unutterable disbelief, Nelson folded his arms. "Have the bos'n pipe the men to the noon meal, and you may forgo the wardroom and dine in your cabin, as you seem to be a hotbed of infestation."

"Aye, sir." He would have taken exception to the captain's smile, were Mark in possession of sufficient faculties to form a suitable rejoinder, but all he could think about was his lady's constancy. "I shall—"

"*Douglas.*"

Again, Mark shot to the fore, as he descended the companionway. "Here."

With a broad grin, the second lieutenant remitted a medium-sized parcel. "Looks like you swept the pool, Mr. Douglas."

"Indeed, it appears so." A tremor of uncontrollable excitement shivered over his flesh when he identified Amanda's handwriting. Mark swaggered two steps and noted a smudge on the brass. With his coat sleeve, he restored the unmarred shine and then spied the boatswain. "Mr. Harker, pipe the men to the noon meal, and Captain has the watch."

"Aye, sir." The boatswain nodded once.

Acknowledging the various salutes offered as he navigated to the mess deck, Mark fought the urge to charge into his cabin, but his heart beat a salvo of delight. Soon, he was lost amid a vortex of anticipation, burning as an unquenchable flame, and passion rode hard in its wake. He entered his cabin, kicked the door shut behind him, deposited his priceless bounty on his bunk, and grinned. "My Amanda, you did not forget me."

At the washstand, he poured water into the basin and then splashed his face. In mere seconds, he doffed his hat, coat, gloves, stock, and boots, before sitting on the bed. Examining his treasure, he arranged the items according to their franking date. Three letters and the box had been posted in December. The two remaining envelopes had been dispatched in January.

Curiosity got the better of him, and he tore into the parcel. As soon as he parted the brown paper, a seductive scent teased his nose, and the signature perfume bathed him in a tidal wave of sumptuous memories. Resting his head against the timbers, Mark closed his eyes and invoked Amanda's image.

He envisioned her in an endless stream of blue velvet gowns, her military-styled pelisse, and her scarlet confection, which had set his blood boiling. But one scene danced at the fringe of his consciousness, ever-present, beckoning as a demanding lover, which refused to be overlooked. It had occurred in the early morning hours in her bedchamber, after he had stoked the flames in the hearth, which had refueled his lady's fire.

Naked and splayed beneath him, with her breasts jostling in time with his thrusts, his Amanda had cast him a shy smile and framed his face. Without care for her own safety, she had aroused, provoked, and then commanded his wild and hedonistic streak, taking unveiled pleasure in his licentious hunger. Heeling his flanks, driving him harder and faster, she had taunted and tempted his barbarian self, until he devoured her. And then, after the sensuous torrent had passed, she held him to her, occasionally kissing his hair, rubbing his scalp, and trailing her fingers on his shoulders. Lying in her arms, Mark had fallen in love with his lady, all over again.

"Oh, sweet Amanda." He groaned, gritted his teeth, and shifted his hips. "How I miss you." Wrenching himself to reality, he opened the oldest letter and laughed.

December 11, 1785
My most cherished, indomitable First Lieutenant,

To say that my heart beats only for you is to diminish the depth of my affection, as I am my beloved's, and my beloved is mine.

"Damn straight, darling." He growled and then read aloud. "At night, I sleep with your pillow, as I have refused to allow Ellie to launder the case, because it smells of my Mark. And I slip between the sheets wearing nothing more than the remembrance of your lips and hands on my body, as I will allow no impediment to the ardent fantasies of you, which haunt my slumber without fail."

After completing the missive, he made short work of the second and third letters, which manifested equal fervor and further stimulated an already vicious erection, and then he returned his attention to the parcel. Inside the box, he found a new pair of pristine gloves and handkerchiefs embroidered with their combined initials, as well as a navy wool scarf and a white waistcoat, the latter two items made by his lady. In an instant, Mark exchanged his garment for hers.

Standing before the small mirror he used for grooming, he turned left and then right, as her hard work had produced an extraordinary fit. And as her note explained, the waistcoat featured an additional inner pocket, sewn over the heart expressly to accommodate her miniature. "Superb, my Amanda. I shall wear it exclusively."

One thing that nagged his conscience was the final statement on the brief correspondence included in the container.

P.S. Why have you not written?

Had he not warned Amanda that the post was erratic at sea? And yet he had endured in his amorous communications. He could only hope that his carefully penned pledges of eternal love reached her, at some point. Then he broke the seal on the fourth envelope.

January 1, 1786
My dearest Mark,

While I understand you labor in the King's service, and I am so very proud of you, I require some sign of your continued persistence, a minor expression, however small, that I remain your beloved. With each passing day, my agony grows, such that I can scarcely maintain my routine. Please, I beg you, as it has been too long. Take pity on my gentle spirit, as it wanes beneath the weight of your indifference. I must know that you are all right.

"Oh, sweetheart." Again and again, he digested the contents of her letter and the palpable desperation underscoring her words. "I could never be indifferent to you."

With a heavy sigh, he glanced at the last unopened envelope and hesitated. Then he speared his fingers through his hair, muttered a curse, cracked the wax seal, unfolded the correspondence—and spiraled into Amanda's pit of melancholy.

January 18, 1786
My beloved Mark,

Am I still your beloved Amanda? Do you pine for me, as I ache for you? Did you receive your Christmas presents? Were the items to your liking? I had thought you might forward even a brief directive in observation of the holidays, yet I have heard nothing from you, despite your promise to write.

Sinking ever deeper into his own hell on earth, Mark whisked a stray tear as he read her detailed events of her family celebrations, struggling to portray an air of genial cordiality, while inside she wallowed in indescribable loss. As he had done with her previous compositions, he recited her penned thoughts. "No longer can I eat or sleep, as my heart bleeds for you. But a single word from you would abolish my misery. How I love you, my darling. I remain, now and forever, your Amanda."

Rubbing his eyes, he stood and then walked to the window, which doubled as a gun portal in battle. Gazing at the eastern sky, Mark swallowed hard. "My Amanda, can you hear me? Can you feel me reaching for you? I am my beloved's, and my beloved is mine. And you are my only love, darling Amanda. Know that when I have my own ship, you shall sail with me, as we are stronger, together. We will marry, my girl, as I will fulfill your father's requirements or die trying."

∽

FEBRUARY ROARED into London in the wake of a crippling snowstorm, which had brought the heart of the British Empire to a crawl. Given the poor road conditions, Amanda's elder sister Olivia, along with her husband Henry and newborn son George, extended their weekend visit. Sitting in the dining room at her family home, Amanda gazed at the dry toast and weak tea positioned before her and blanched.

"Amanda, you will eat your meal." Her father pounded his fist on the table. "I have had enough of your nonsense."

With nary a missive from her beloved Mark, she wallowed in a seemingly endless pit of desolation and despair. The greater portion of her days she spent locked in her room, knitting scarves for her charity, unable to sleep or take sustenance, as whatever she consumed she soon revisited. And while her lieutenant had remarked on the capricious nature of the post, she should have received something from him by January, or so she thought.

"Leave her be, Hiram." Her mother sniffed. "After all, *you* broke her heart."

"Eleanor, I did no such thing." Papa set down his fork, and Amanda braced for the argument she knew was forthcoming, as her parents bickered constantly, in light of her sire's inexplicable actions regarding her betrothal, the motives of which he steadfastly refused to divulge. "I issued my requirements, which young Douglas will either fulfill or fail."

"May I be excused?" A familiar knot settled in her belly, and Amanda fought encroaching nausea.

"Yes."

"No."

"Of course, you may retire, my darling girl." Mama smiled. "I shall send up Ellie with a fresh pot of tea."

"Thank you, Mama." Amanda stood.

"Does no one abide my edicts anymore?" Her father frowned and snorted. "Am I not head of this household? Does no one listen to me?"

"Not until you have something worthwhile to contribute to the conversation." With that, Mama tossed her napkin to her plate, eased back her chair, and rose from her seat. "Come, Olivia. Let us leave the men to their cigars, brandy, and vastly superior dialogue."

"Hold hard, little one." In the hall, Olivia caught Amanda by the wrist. "Wait for me in your chamber, as I have something important for you."

"Of course." Intrigued, Amanda nodded once and hurried upstairs. In her sitting room, she sank to the *chaise* and twisted the engraved band on her finger. As always, images from that spectacular night flooded her consciousness, and she swayed with heady excitement.

Then she plucked a satin covered box from the table and lifted the lid. Inside, cradled in a puff of white cotton, rested a sterling silver holiday ornament, engraved with the phrase, *Our First Christmas, 1785*. The Yule decoration, which had been purchased as a celebration of her union with Mark, now served as a painful reminder of their separation. With a mournful exhalation, she abandoned the parcel.

"Alone, at last, little sister." Olivia locked the door and then scurried forth. "These arrived only this afternoon, and Mama bade me hide them from Papa, as he has been entirely unreasonable where your Lieutenant Douglas is concerned."

"*Oh*." With a squeal of delight mixed with relief, Amanda grabbed the bound collection of envelopes, bearing instantly recognizable military franking. Clutching the precious, much-prayed-for-correspondence to her chest, she sank amid the cushions. "They are from Mark."

"I suspected as much." Olivia sat beside Amanda and slipped an arm about her shoulders. "I am so sorry Papa placed conditions on your betrothal, but I am not surprised, as he made Henry wait six months for our nuptials, and my husband is an earl. My what a charming ring. Where did you get it?"

"It is from my beloved, and I shall never take it off." In that instant, the tension holding her prisoner yielded to the sorrow over her predicament, and the damn burst. Resting in her sister's embrace, Amanda wept and sobbed without shame. "I swear if Mark is injured, or worse, I will never forgive Papa."

"Poor gadling." Olivia rocked and crooned in a gentle rhythm. "There, there, dearest. You have had a terrible time of it, but your lieutenant sends proof of his regard, so you must rejoice and rally. And has Papa disclosed his requirements for his consent?"

"I know, and I cannot wait to read his letters." She scanned the dispatch dates, which spanned the length of their separation. "I should have known he had not forgot me. My love warned me that the post was unreliable at sea, but I feared something terrible had happened. And Papa will not tell me what he requires, and he made Mark promise to keep it secret, which, to my frustration, my beau obeyed."

"Then I should abandon you to your task, but I have something else to impart, which may allay your concerns." Olivia revealed a red velvet pouch, along with a leather-bound journal. "Mama gave this to me the night Papa announced my engagement. She was unsure of my devotion to Henry and our determination to wed, and she wanted me to be certain of my chosen mate."

"What is it?" Amanda held up her hand and accepted into her palm a curious piece of jewelry, which Olivia deposited from the nondescript purse. "How lovely."

Turning the unique item in her grasp, she studied the face and the underside. Fashioned of old gold, the simple but remarkable egg-shaped lady's badge boasted four round rubies and a large oval-cut sapphire. Ornate, if ancient, craftsmanship bespoke a master goldsmith, as intricate etching, which featured a lotus blossom and a lotus in buds, rendered the otherwise ordinary brooch quite extraordinary.

"It belonged to our ancestors, and as the oldest, I am to pass it down to my first daughter," Olivia explained. "But nothing says I cannot loan it to you, now, so you may benefit from its influence. According to lore, the wearer of the brooch will dream of her true love. It worked for Mama, as well as I."

"Pull my other leg." Amanda emitted a half-suppressed laugh, even as her suspicions roused, and she was tempted. "What game are you about, sister?"

"No, you mistake my intent, as I am serious." Olivia opened the old tome. "See? It says right here, 'Ye lady what dons this brooch of ethereal sight, shall enjoy unfettered dreams of her one true knight.'"

"And the entries describe what the brooch revealed to

various women, over the years. This is fascinating." Amanda flipped through the parchment, yellowed with age, and located her sibling's notation at the end. "You envisioned Henry's signet ring?"

"Yes." With a watery gaze, Olivia dipped her chin. "Every night, without fail, I saw his signet ring, before I ever knew it existed, and I realized, without the slightest bit of skepticism, I had made the right choice. Never have I doubted Henry's love, and I would give you the same peace of mind, little sister."

"Thank you, but I require no antique artifact to discern that Mark is my future husband." Amanda recalled the heated consummation of their tender pledge, and her cheeks burned as fierce as the memory. "In fact, in our perspective, we are already married."

"I do not believe it." With mouth agape, Olivia stood. "You dallied with Lieutenant Douglas." It was a statement, not a question.

"I beg your pardon?" Amanda gulped, as she had no plans to reveal that scrap of information. "I have done no—"

"Please, do not insult my intelligence or my eyes with denial." She settled hands on hips and shifted her weight. "I am a happily wedded wife, with an equally attentive husband, and I know the signs. Are you with child? Is that the cause of your stomach ailment, of late?"

"No, I am not pregnant." In desperate search of distraction, Amanda commenced a more careful appraisal of the brooch.

"Are you positive?" Olivia tapped an impatient cadence with her slippered foot. "You had better be sure, as Papa will kill you and Douglas."

"Yes, I am certain, because my courses have flowed twice since he departed London." Amanda sniffed. "Much to my disappointment."

Loving Lieutenant Douglas 91

"Upon my word, but you do astonish me. So you gifted him your maidenhead?" Olivia inquired in a small voice.

Incapable of speech, she nodded her confirmation.

"How I wish you had talked with me prior to embarking on such ambitious stratagem, as I could have provided useful insight and instruction. Although Mama detailed what I could expect of the consummation, I am left to presume she could never fathom the capacity for passion my Henry possesses." To Amanda's infinite shock, her sister returned to the *chaise*. "Were you frightened? Did he hurt you—well, beyond the obvious?"

"Oh, Olivia." Dying to share her experience with someone, Amanda smiled and pressed a clenched fist to her breast. "Mark was wonderful—amazing, so thoughtful and gentle, yet he was —*oh*, I know not how to describe it."

"Did he curl your toes?" With an arched brow, Olivia giggled.

"He curled everything." She closed her eyes and sighed, as she recalled the breathtaking pinnacle of their nocturnal maneuvers. "I get gooseflesh just thinking of him."

"I believe that bodes well for your union." Olivia cupped Amanda's cheek and then her older sister averted her gaze. "And I must confess a secret, given your candor, and yet I know I can trust you to maintain my confidence, as we are a pair. While everyone fretted over George's early arrival, my son was, in fact, right on time."

"No." Amanda gasped and squeezed her sister's fingers. "You mean you and Henry—"

"Indeed." Olivia tittered. "Several times, as we could not wait, so I understand your actions, sweet Amanda. And, like your Mark, my Henry is a most considerate lover."

"Is it not good fortune, for both our sakes?" Now Amanda wanted to cry, as the unimaginable happiness associated with thoughts of Mark, absent of late, resurfaced with a vengeance. "I mean the *ton* is littered with indifferent husbands, and we found two such estimable men."

"Yes, we are most blessed." Olivia slid from the *chaise* and surveyed the room. "You have made quite a few changes to the décor, since you moved into my old apartments, and the color suits you. I have countless fond memories in these chambers, many of which involve suspect use of the trellis, just outside that window."

"What?" Amanda reflected on their conversation, pictured Mark's perilous descent, and then flinched. "You and Henry—here?"

"Need I remind you that Papa made us wait six months to marry? You and I have more in common than you realize, as it appears that bed has seen more action than the legendary Captain Nelson. Now, you will want to read your letters, so I shall take my leave, but know that I am always here for you." Olivia strolled to the door but paused. "And when next your lieutenant returns to our shores, impart a bit of sage advice intended to save the neck of my future brother-in-law. Tell him to use the center rungs, as Henry had them reinforced, without Papa's notice, after my groom took a nasty spill."

Amanda burst into laughter.

Then Olivia winked and exited, and Amanda gave her full attention to the envelopes resting in her lap. Of the seven, she noticed one had been dispatched only a sennight ago, and she ripped into the most current missive.

February 2, 1786
My darling Amanda,
While I pen this brief note, as a Packet Ship waits, and I dare not tarry, I am most aggrieved. Having received your letters and Christmas gifts, for which I am infinitely grateful, I am distressed by your lack of care for your person, which I hold so dear, and doubts

concerning the constancy of my affection, which remains unchanged from our last meeting. Has the post not delivered my correspondence, faithfully dispatched, as promised? Given our separation, which I suffer as a grave wound, my love grows more fervent with each passing day, and I count the hours until I see you again. When I dock in London, and we are reunited, I shall leave you in no uncertainty regarding my ardent admiration. Like fifty men, sweetheart. But as that happy time remains unfixed, I would ask a favor. Once the sun sinks below the yardarm, locate the North Star in the night sky, and know that I will do the same, every evening, without fail, as that is the closest I may come to your embrace. Remember, I am my beloved's, and my beloved is mine.

Forever, your Mark

Amanda peered out the window, as twilight fast approached. In a flash, she tossed aside the sheaf of letters and the brooch and ran into the hall. Veering left, she soared down the back stairs and charged into the morning room. At the terrace doors, she gazed at the heavens. Recalling what her father had taught her about navigation and the constellations, she identified the North Star and all but bounced with excitement.

"Oh, Mark. How I love you." Wrapping her arms about herself, she willed him to hear her declaration. "And I vow I will marry you, or I shall die a spinster."

CHAPTER SEVEN

The first shot across the bow brought the *Boreas* hard a-larboard, and Mark slammed into the wall, as he attempted to exit his cabin. In mid-February, the ship had been re-tasked to the Antiguas to enforce the Navigation Acts, which were unpopular, to say the least, with Americans and privateers, so the attack came as no surprise.

As the boards rumbled beneath his feet, he stumbled to the gun deck and then crawled up the companionway to the waist. When the ship pitched hard a-starboard, he rolled into the rail and used it as a ladder, of sorts, to gain the quarterdeck. At the helm, Captain Nelson barked one order after another, and Mark shuffled left and then right, as men of the watch scrambled in all directions.

"Ah, Mr. Douglas." Captain Nelson peered through his spyglass. "She bears down with ports open, as a provocative invitation. What action would you suggest?"

Puzzled by Nelson's odd request, as the venerable naval legend required no such advice, Mark leveled the bring-em-closer and focused. "She looks familiar."

"You have a good eye, Mr. Douglas," Nelson stated with

unimpaired aplomb and chucked Mark's shoulder, as the vessel shook violently. "And where do you suppose you have seen her?"

"She is a thirty-six-gun, *Perseverance*-class frigate, with eighteen-pounders, sir." He knew her, all right. And then a tremor of recognition jolted his hearty frame. "Bloody hell, she is the *Inconstant*."

"Correction. She was the *Inconstant*, taken by the Americans during their revolution and, so it appears, now persists in the hands of pirates," Nelson stated with an air of grim finality. "Such a sad sight. And yet we can only imagine the gratitude displayed by a most indebted Admiralty upon learning that you have reclaimed her."

"What?" Mark snapped to attention. "You wish me to board her?"

"How else might you seize your first command, Mr. Douglas?" Nelson inquired calmly and then arched a brow. "Do you or do you not wish to make post?"

Then the logic behind his captain's motives dawned, and Mark smiled with confidence. "Aye, sir."

"Mr. Eccleston, draw the guns and load with grape, as we shall not strike her hull, but you may sweep the deck. Sharpshooters to the tunnels." So dedicated to his duty, Nelson had not so much as flinched, when another premature blast sent water spraying over the helm. "Mr. Pelham, topsails and forecourse, only. And Mr. Douglas, prepare your assault for the broadside."

"What is your plan, Captain?" Mark formulated an invasion, as the second and third lieutenants conveyed the orders. To win, he would need to move swift and sure.

"She will wager everything on a single barrage." Nelson inclined his head and narrowed his stare. "So I should heel hard a-port, bump her bows, and come aft."

"Then the lobsters should muster to board over her bow." Mark posited additional strategy in silence. "And I should target her quarterdeck."

"Very good, Mr. Douglas." Nelson snickered. "And I shall bestow upon you the temporary rank of Lieutenant-Commander by sunset."

"Then I must return to my cabin and fetch my pistols, sir." He saluted. "With your permission."

"As you were." Nelson dipped his chin. "Sharply, Mr. Douglas."

With that, Mark retraced his steps in an awkward dance with the motion of the rocking ship. In his quarters, he donned his finest coat, retrieved and checked his weapons, and then he drew Amanda's portrait from his waistcoat pocket.

"I do this for us, darling." His kissed her image, set the miniature on the table, made for the door, but reversed course. Grasping the sapphire and pearl encrusted gold frame, he re-tucked the small painting in the breast pocket of the waistcoat his lady had made just for him. "Either we succeed or go down, together, my love."

In mere minutes he rejoined the men at the waist, where the Marines and the Boreans had assembled, and an eerie quiet fell over the group. The northeast trades whispered and thrummed through the rigging, in a morose audial tapestry, and the crew stationed at the guns. Tension invested the motley band of brothers, as the stakes were great. On the quarterdeck, Nelson directed the helmsman, and the *Boreas* heeled hard a-port.

Gazing at the sky, Mark uttered a silent prayer that he might keep his evening date with his Amanda and the North Star. Never before had he pondered the future on the precipice of close action, but never had so much depended on the outcome, as Amanda was his to win or lose. Then he closed his eyes, as his heart beat a salvo in his ears, and he invoked the guileless reflection of his lady.

In his reverie, she glowed with effuse ebullience, as she extended her arms and reached for him. Inhaling a deep breath, he imagined her dainty hands cupping his face, as she pressed her lips to his, and he could almost taste her intoxicating sweetness. At last, his pulse slowed, and he rolled his shoulders and relaxed. Buoyed with renewed strength and determination, he lowered his chin and stared at his prize.

"Stand by to board." Nelson assessed their position, as the deck shuddered. "*Fire!*" Before the pirates could respond with an additional cannonade, Nelson ranged up the *Boreas*, and the two ships came to rest, side by side.

"And Marines away." Mark charged aft, swung through the shrouds, and launched to the enemy craft. With his sword drawn, he severed the boarding-netting, to a hailstorm of cheering Boreans—and the fight commenced.

Musket-fire echoed, as the Marines charged the waist. On the quarterdeck, Mark shot a menacing pirate and struck another with the hilt of his sword. The enemy rallied and charged, and sunlight glittered on the flat of the blades, as all hell broke loose.

"Advance, Marines. Boreans, take the companionway to the gun deck." In the lead, Mark confronted two villains, one considerably larger than the other. Given the choice, he pulled the second pistol from his waistband, dispatched the bigger of the duo, and challenged the remaining foe. "You there, *en garde*."

"Lieutenant, watch out." A soldier punched a shaggy-haired scoundrel, which had flanked Mark, as if from nowhere.

Weaving left and then right, he pushed forward. After slicing the blackguard across the forearm, Mark stuck the pirate between the ribs and moved to his next target. With a wave, he shouted, "Onward, Boreans. Make haste, make haste, as we must secure the guns."

A sharp assessment revealed His Majesty's soldiers and sailors far outpaced the privateers, in numbers, ordnance, and skill. But the enemy adhered not to the Articles of War, so they were ruthless in their tactics and unpredictability. When a foe leaped from a well-situated hiding place, Mark drew short. To his good fortune, he found a discarded pistol, picked it up, and pulled the trigger, felling the would-be assassin.

On the gun deck, the Marines had assumed command and quartered a pack of pirates, dispirited and sullen, as they had surrendered. With the eighteen-pounders in friendly hands, Mark guided his men, running fast and furious, down the gangway, which was spattered with blood and littered with corpses, to the mess deck for a final assault. As he had presumed, the last of the pirates had chosen the bowels of the ship to make their stand.

"Follow me." Again, Mark charged the fray without hesitance.

The lanterns had been doused, and it seemed villains lunged from all directions, springing from the shadows in some sort of macabre gambol. Mark deflected a blade and turned aside another, but the sword slashed through his coat sleeve and his flesh, and he winced but remained steadfast. When a buccaneer caught Mark unaware, landing a blow to his jaw, he stumbled backwards, tripped over a body, but recovered and progressed, dispatching the combatant in the process.

"The hold, waist, and gun deck has been cleared, sir." A Marine lieutenant emerged from behind, with a platoon of lobsters to offer support.

"Then position your soldiers." Mark bashed the head of a particularly persistent privateer and then stepped aside. "Aim sharply, men. *Fire*."

Gunfire rent the air, as the smell of powder weighed heavy in his nostrils, and Mark choked on the acrid smoke. But the last of the bandits yielded and surrendered their armaments. In the wardroom, a swarthy but clean-shaven pirate held high a ceremonial sword, which Mark suspected was stolen.

"The ship is yours, sir." The blackguard scowled. "But I would have your word that my men will be treated fairly."

"On my honor, you and your crew shall be handled according to the Articles of War, until we reach London, and you are remanded into custody, sir." Mark spat blood, which had seeped from his injured lip. "Lieutenant Sharpe, secure the prisoners in the hold, as a makeshift guardhouse, and post a watch to rotate on the bells."

"Aye, sir." Sharpe dipped his chin and then elbowed Mark in the ribs. "Congratulations, Mr. Douglas."

"Thank you, Lieutenant." Riding a swell of pride unlike any he had ever known, Mark all but skipped up the gangway. When he emerged on the quarterdeck, he shifted his weight and then thrust the ceremonial sword overhead. A thunderous roar erupted on both vessels, and Mark cursed the mortifying burn of a blush.

"Ahoy." Captain Nelson saluted, which Mark returned, measure for measure. "Well done, Mr. Douglas. What is the butcher's bill?"

"It appears we lost three marines and two sailors, sir." He rubbed his now sore jaw. "The pirates suffered twenty-three casualties and half as many injuries."

"Fine work, Mr. Douglas." Nelson folded his arms. "I should compose a report, along with temporary orders, so you may depart for London, posthaste. And evaluate your stores, as we should transfer the necessary supplies to ensure your safe journey."

"Yes, Captain." Mark appraised the helm and then flagged a

soldier. "Have Lieutenant Sharpe conduct a thorough search of the ship, as we should beware of snipers."

"An excellent notion, Mr. Douglas." The soldier clicked his heels and saluted.

With a sigh of relief, Mark glanced at the ever-darkening sky and shimmering twilight. Locating the North Star, he smiled.

Well, we have done it, my girl. And you had better fortify yourself, because I am coming for you like fifty men.

With naughty thoughts of Lady Amanda, warm and inviting on his wedding night, swirling in his brain, he turned just as a pirate sprang from behind a stack of lashed barrels, leveled a pistol, took careful aim, and shot Mark in the chest.

∼

"*No.*" Amanda lurched upright in bed and gasped for air. It took a few seconds to discern she remained in her chamber, safe and sound. In a moment of raw frustration, she ripped the ancient brooch from her bodice, which tore the material, and threw the pin across the room. "I will marry my lieutenant, or I shall never wed."

In the world beyond the windows, the seasons changed, the birds sang, and the roses bloomed, as winter yielded to spring. March had exited with an impressive gale, which matched her mood—wild, unpredictable, and sybaritic. But for Amanda, her existence had devolved into a dull routine spent primarily in her apartments, knitting scarves for her charity and lamenting the seemingly endless absence of her beloved Mark.

Only the occasional arrival of his correspondence, which the post delivered in fits and starts, allayed her torment, but she had received nothing since the first of April, and her concern for his welfare had increased by epic proportions. It was, perhaps, the insipid regimen, coupled with intense vexation, that had tempted her to nap, every afternoon, without fail, for the past sennight, with the curious piece of jewelry, loaned by her sister, attached to her garments. And to her everlasting shock and heartbreak, the same vision taunted her slumber without mercy.

"I do not care what you show me. Now and forever, I belong to Mark." She glared at the gold bauble, resting on the floor where it landed, as if expecting it to respond to her proclamation. A knock at the door to her sitting room had her leaping from the bed. "Come."

"Good evening, my dear." Carrying a large box, Papa entered. "Where is Ellie, and why are you not preparing for my birthday celebration?"

"Because I refuse to attend any party, until Mark returns to London." She averted her gaze and sniffed. "I believe I have made my preference known since the start of the Season, sir."

"Yes, I am well acquainted with your stubborn streak, which I have indulged to the point of madness. But you will attend our fête." He caught her in a lethal stare. "And as you scarcely have been out of the house, since the holidays, I have taken the liberty of procuring an outfit for the special occasion. So summon your lady's maid, this instant."

"I will not." She folded her arms, as her father set the parcel on the *chaise*.

"Amanda Catherine, while you may slight me and rain any number of curses on my head, you will not offend our guests." Papa sighed, tugged the bell pull, which signaled Ellie, and then reversed course. At the entry, he said, "Now, if you do not present yourself at the receiving line, promptly at six, I will drag you downstairs, in whatever state I find you, so you had better think twice before defying me. Do I make myself clear?"

"Yes, sir." For a minute, she considered flouting her sire's order, but she knew from past experience he would make good on his threat, so she walked to the *chaise* and lifted the lid on the container. Her chest seized, her gut clenched, and her ears pealed a *soupçon* of alarm. "Oh, no."

The navy silk gown boasted a fitted bodice trimmed in gold piping, along with three rows of gold buttons, set at equal distances. But it was the gold braiding located at the cuffs of the long sleeves that manifested the source of her distress, because their distinct pattern had haunted her naps for the last week. The captain's regalia of which she had dreamed bespoke the rank of her one true knight and future husband, according to the associative lore.

"If Papa attempts to betroth me to anyone but my lieutenant, I shall flee to the Continent," she vowed, with a clenched fist pressed to her bosom. And then she ran to the window and pressed her forehead to the glass. "Oh, Mark. Please, come back to me."

"You rang, my lady?" Ellie skipped to the fore. "I say, what a lovely dress, and it is done in your customary military flair. You will be the talk of the ball. Perhaps I should arrange your hair in a loose chignon with a curl draped at your throat."

"That sounds perfect, Ellie." Resolved to persevere, Amanda sat at her vanity and studied her reflection, as her lady's maid coiffed her black locks to perfection. Girded for the showdown she suspected awaited her in the ballroom, she pledged to stand firm in her position, as no captain, however impressive, could take her from Mark. At last, she clutched the maid's hand. "Thank you, my dear friend. Your unwavering support, throughout the years, has meant more than you know. Now, help me into the gown."

"Yes, my lady." Ellie curtseyed and then fetched Papa's gift.

Even as Ellie tied the laces, Amanda scrutinized the festooned cuffs, which portended nefarious enterprises, and she wanted nothing more than to rip the garment to shreds. After a last check in the long mirror, she marched into the hall and trudged down the stairs. In the foyer, she stood beside her mother.

"Dearest, how charming you look." Mama kissed Amanda's cheek. "And I am so happy you chose to join us, tonight."

"Papa left me no alternative." She refused to acknowledge her father. "And so I am here, but I partake of the events under duress, and I am determined not to enjoy the party."

"Well, I believe by the end of the night, you shall sing another tune." Her mother smiled, and Amanda swallowed hard. "Because cousin Helen here."

"Oh." Amanda sighed in relief. At last she gained a coconspirator who understood the situation. "It seems ages since we last met."

"My big toe, how it ails me, what with all the blasted rain." Helen elbowed Amanda from behind. "And what manner of mischief has kept you from my doorstep, little one?"

"Most favorite cousin." In dire need of reinforcement, Amanda hugged her brash relation. "How I have missed you."

"Stuff and nonsense, as you should have visited me." Helen snorted and grasped Amanda's chin. "And what have you done to yourself?"

"I beg your pardon?" Amanda curled her toes in her slippers, as her cousin narrowed her stare. "I have done nothing. In fact, most of my time is spent in my chambers."

"Are you trying to knit enough scarves for the entire military population? I suppose that explains why you are pale as a ghost." Arm in arm, Helen positioned herself in the receiving line to Amanda's left. "And what will your young man say when he sees you?"

"Given I have not enjoyed his company since December, and I have no idea when Mark will return to our shores, much to my dismay, what have I to worry?" That she might waste away? That he might not recognize what remained of her if he ever made it home? That she might die of heartbreak before she reached her nineteenth year? "But I am sorry I have neglected you, as that was never my intent."

"I understand that, but you cannot fool me, cousin, as I was not born yesterday." Helen chuckled. "You seek to punish your father, yet you only injure yourself and your sailor, as Douglas will not approve your methods, especially when he notes those black circles beneath your eyes."

"But it is not my fault." As the first guests had arrived, Amanda whispered, "I cannot eat or sleep, as fear of the unknown holds me prisoner to the most horrible thoughts."

"Good evening, Lady Amanda." Captain Brent Randolph, along with his wife, Lady Elizabeth, smiled. "It is fortunate you regained sufficient health to attend tonight's festivities, as the *ton's* ballrooms have suffered your absence, my dear."

"And what a unique gown." Lady Beth admired the gold braiding on the cuffs. "Why it is the captain's insignia, and how appropriate—"

"Uh—darling, let us not monopolize Lady Amanda, as she has been unwell." Captain Randolph ushered his wife down the line.

Nagging suspicion settled as the weight of the world on Amanda's shoulders, as she digested Lady Beth's comment and her husband's reaction. Had Papa arranged a marriage, the news of which he had shared with his closest friends and planned to announce at his birthday celebration? If so, then he sported for disappointment, because that was one gift she would not grant him.

The grand ballroom at her family's London residence boasted floor to ceiling oak panels in the *Boiserie* style, by François-Joseph Bélanger, and Austrian crystal chandeliers. As the cavernous structure filled with one hundred of her father's closest connections, both friends and family, Amanda galvanized her commitment to Mark, and she would not waver. When the orchestra struck the initial notes of a waltz, Papa sought her partnership for the first dance, and she knew, without doubt, there were games afoot.

"Shall we, my child?" His cherubic countenance left her reeling, and she teetered and stumbled. "Hold hard, Amanda. Are you infirm?"

"No, Papa." They assumed their respective positions, and she averted her gaze, until he twisted the gold band on her finger, and she gulped.

"What an interesting ring, and you opt for an intriguing placement." Papa arched a brow and frowned. "Where did you get it, or need I inquire?"

"If you must know, Mark gave it to me—before you sent him away." She humphed. "And I shall be buried with it, as never will it leave my person."

"Is that the way the wind blows?" Papa whirled her with an uncharacteristic flourish. "Are you of a single-mind?"

"Indeed, I am so fixed." How sad it was that the one man she had always counted an ally now stood as her greatest foe and impediment to her dreams. "And I will not relent, regardless of arguments to the contrary."

"And what of me?" He reversed course without missing a step. "Do my wishes mean nothing?"

"I would ask the same of you, sir," quick as a wink she replied. "What of my wishes, or do they not signify because they conflict with yours?"

"You are your mother's daughter. Obstinate, inflexible girl." And then he shocked her with a full belly laugh. "But I am not surprised. So, tell me, does the strapping Douglas mean that much to you?"

"He is my life, Papa." In that she had not lied, because she saw no future without Mark. "I will have no other."

"All right." He narrowed his stare. "And you are certain it is not merely a crush or a flighty fancy, which—"

"It is neither a crush nor a fancy, and you insult me with such absurd assertions." She lifted her chin. "I love Lieutenant Douglas, and he owns me, body and soul."

"Even after these months apart?" Papa inclined his head. "And smile, else you will announce our contretemps to the guests and embarrass our family."

Amanda bared her teeth. "Even more so, after these months apart."

"Strong words." Her father compressed his lips. "And you cannot be dissuaded?"

"I know no other language, when it comes to my heart." Somehow, she had to make him understand her perspective and devotion. "And I will not yield."

"Well said, yet I expected no less." He opened and then closed his mouth. "My dear, have you not wondered at my reasons for delaying your engagement?"

"Of course, but you have refused to enlighten me, and Mark has steadfastly maintained your confidence in his letters." Much to her frustration, which she would take up with him when next they met. "So I am to guess."

"No, you need not postulate, as I would explain myself." Again, he twirled her, as Mama encouraged the guests to merge on the dance floor, and the orchestra transitioned into a second waltz. "You see my aim was to test the mettle of your prospective bridegroom, as I could not relinquish you, my pride and joy, to just anyone."

"What?" In her befuddlement, she tripped, but her sire kept her upright. "Oh, Papa, you must know that Mark is most deserving."

"Of that, I have no doubt." Now Papa chucked her chin. "But I had to gauge his capacity for discretion, even under the most trying circumstances, and neither could I forfeit you to a minor lieutenant, as I have great plans for him."

"Do you?" Stunned, she blinked. "So you approve his suit? You will allow us to marry?"

"As I promised your estimable lieutenant, I shall consent when he meets the whole of my conditions." He chuckled when she squealed with arrant delight. "Am I to understand I have, at last, made you happy?"

In answer to his query, Amanda hugged her father, and she relaxed, when he lifted her from her feet and carried her about the rotation, as he had when she was but a child. And then he hummed with the lilting movement, as he had done on many a night, at her bedside, evoking fond memories of carefree times.

"Papa, I do love you." Tears threatened, and she willed herself to remain calm. "And I am sorry we quarreled."

"It is all right, girl." When the music ended, he eased his hold and then kissed her forehead. "Have faith in Douglas, as I believe he will satisfy you. Now savor the fête, as the night is young."

With that, she recalled her evening ritual, her date with Mark and the North Star. After a quick curtsey, Amanda weaved through the throng until she reached the back wall. Peering out the window, she discovered her err in orientation and hurried to the correct bearing. And then she spied what she had come to think of as their star, twinkling as a beacon of hope for the prospects she desperately desired.

"Oh, my darling." She pressed her nose to the glass. "How I miss you."

"Talking to yourself?" Helen chortled and shifted her weight. "Or have you completely lost your head over Douglas?"

"Hush, cousin." Gazing at the sky, and sending private and inappropriate thoughts to her man, she refused to be baited or distracted. "I have a very important assignation, which you cannot fathom."

"With a particular sailor?" Helen clucked her tongue.

"Yes." She pictured him as he had loomed at the base of the trellis, and she uttered his name in silence. Was there anything so sad as watching a loved one walk away?

"I suppose your separation must be difficult to endure," Helen remarked with unmasked sympathy.

"More than you can apprehend, unless you have survived similar circumstances." Was he somewhere on the deep blue sea, perusing their star at that instant?

"So you are most anxious to be reunited." Helen gave Amanda a gentle nudge. "You still fancy him?"

"Of course." She rested her chin on her clasped hands. "And I love Mark."

"Then you look in the wrong direction, little one." Helen grabbed Amanda by the shoulders and whirled her about to face the gala. "As it appears we have a late arrival."

The world rocked beneath her feet, and she tensed. Standing in the entranceway, tall, sun-kissed, and gorgeous, wearing regimentals that bore braided regalia identical to that of her gown, her beloved scanned the crowd. When their eyes met, he favored her with a slow, sensual smile, and Amanda all but screamed, "*Mark.*"

CHAPTER EIGHT

The music died, as Amanda shrieked his name, and a murmur built, low at first but increasing as incoming tidewater. Captain Mark Douglas splayed his arms wide in welcome. To his absolute delight, his lady started in his direction with unveiled enthusiasm. By her second step, she had hiked her skirts in a scandalous display of her calves, broken into a full sprint, and the crowd parted to permit her passage. When she leaped, he caught her, mid-air, and she showered his face in sweet kisses.

"Er—Amanda." He cast a side-glance at her father, who appeared none too pleased by his daughter's unabashed ardor. "Darling, we are in mixed company."

"I do not care, as I missed you terribly." And then she framed his cheeks and pressed her lips to his.

Mark should have chastised his lady, regarding her gross breach in etiquette, should have shown restraint and set an example, should have resisted her untutored but nonetheless potent advances, yet his heretofore vaunted discipline, which had vanquished untold enemies in the heat of battle, conceded to the sheer power of her unchecked desire. And, heaven help him, he was hungry.

The gentlemen chuckled, and the ladies giggled, in a comedic chorale.

"Take her to my study and calm her." The marquess wrenched Mark. "And be quick about it, as we shall make the announcement just prior to dinner."

Given his society maiden's outright refusal to release him, he managed a half-nod, tightened his arms at her waist, and carried her from the gala, across the foyer, into a side hall, and entered the man's domain he remembered so well. Considering Amanda's propensity to defeat his defenses, he locked the door before easing his hold.

And then Mark made a series of inappropriate maneuvers of his own; as he cupped her bottom, thrust his hips, and slaked his aching arousal in the softness of her belly. Angling his head, he assumed control and claimed her mouth, nipping and suckling her sumptuous flesh, and her moan well nigh slayed him. It had been too long since he had tasted her.

"Where have you been, when did you return to London, and why have you not paid call?" Breathing heavily, she rested her forehead to his. "How I have yearned for you."

True to form, she embarked on an interrogation, neither frivolous nor consequential, and ended with an expression of affection, and he could only laugh at her haughty demeanor. "Oh, my Amanda, I have endured your absence as the cruelest cut to the heart since the morning I stood at the base of your window and bade you farewell."

With a squeal, she charged with the force of an entire brigade, and he stumbled and tripped backwards until he dropped into a large chair. And to her credit, she never allowed a hairsbreadth of distance between them, as she hitched her skirts and straddled his thighs.

Advantageously situated, he at last partook an unfettered examination of his lady, and what he spied gave him immediate cause for concern, as no endearing blush invested her cheeks. Instead, her complexion had paled, dark circles framed her blue eyes, and she appeared thinner.

"You have waned, love." He tipped her chin. "Have you been ill?"

"Yes, for want of you, and I simply cannot bear it." She scored her nails to the nape of his neck. "And once we are married I wish never to be separated from you again, so you will take me with you when next you sail."

"Ah, there is my officious little thing." Of course, Mark would not admit he had already arrived at the same conclusion, as he knew from past experience he could not allow her so much sway. "Amanda, I should warn you life is hard at sea."

"I care not, as long as I am with you." She nuzzled his temple. "As the days are far more difficult without you."

"And it is dangerous." Perhaps it was a bit of fortunate foresight he had hired a tradesman to install an extra large bunk, and a tub that would accommodate two, in his new cabin.

"What have I to fear, with you at my side?" Amanda caught the crest of his ear with her teeth.

"I must maintain ruthless control and discipline aboard ship." Jolly Roger, excluded, because his overly jolly Roger had just run up the colors. "You must abide my dictates, without question."

"I shall obey your every command." She unbuttoned his coat and waistcoat. "You need but convey your directives."

"I like the sound of that." He groaned, as she shifted, but it was too late when he discerned her intent. Before he realized it, she had unhooked his breeches, positioned herself, and eased her body down, cocooning his rock-solid length in her warmth, in much the same fashion as she had enacted their first union. "Bloody hell, Amanda."

"Please, do not scold me, as I need you." The relief in her countenance halted his reproach, and then she danced as he had taught her on that magnificent night.

So Mark reclined in the chair, let her have her way, and she rode him hell-bent for leather into voluptuous oblivion. And in the dark recesses of his mind still capable of coherent thought, he wondered if there were anything so erotic as his bride-to-be in the throes of passion.

It seemed as blissful hours, but in reality only a handful of minutes had passed in heated, panting, lustful, intensely silent endeavors. When Mark surfaced from a gut-wrenching climax, he discovered his lady collapsed against his chest.

"That ought to give you something to ponder as you negotiate our marriage contract with Papa—*ouch*." With a frown, she propped herself and then retrieved her miniature from his pocket. "Oh, no. What happened to my portrait?"

"It is a long story." One he had not planned to share just yet.

"I am rather fond of long stories," she replied in a small voice. "And I have an awful feeling."

So despite preferences otherwise, he detailed the events of the boarding, as well as the ensuing melee. But he would not ruin the special occasion, which he had carefully plotted with her father. "My dear, we should return to the party."

"Not until you explain the dent in the frame." She sat upright.

"Amanda—"

"Now." With arms folded, she seemed completely impervious to the fact that she still held his flesh deep within hers.

"After the pirates had surrendered, I gathered my officers on the quarterdeck to issue orders." Mark braced for her response.

"Without warning, a sniper jumped from behind a barrel and shot me."

"What?" She tensed around him, and he gritted his teeth, as the cannon in his crotch reloaded and primed for a second assault.

He grimaced. "There is no need to overreact, because your gift deflected the ball, and—"

"I am not overreacting." She clutched the lapels of his coat. "And I would have the whole of it, sir."

"The blackguard had a deuced fine aim." He speared his fingers through his hair. "He struck me in the chest, but your talisman guarded my heart in more ways than one. You saved my life, darling."

In that instant, she unfastened his shirt and gasped when her gaze lit upon what remained of the nasty bruise, which had faded considerably in the brief six weeks it had taken him to sail to London, because he had kept the canvas hardened in and shaved a sennight off the usual journey. Tracing the outline of his injury, she met his stare, and a tear coursed her cheek.

"We are not at war, and you could have been killed." Amanda sniffed. "What on earth possessed you to undertake such dangerous actions?"

"It was the only means to make post." With his thumb he trailed the gentle curve of her jawline.

"And that matters?" She rested her head on his shoulder, skimmed the lawn, and pressed her palm to his skin. "I would have married you as a lieutenant, as I care not for your rank."

"Thank you, sweetheart." He kissed her hair. "But your father required I promote as his primary stipulation to bless our betrothal."

"And yet his precondition could have landed you in a premature grave." She snaked her arms about his waist and squeezed.

"True." He hissed as she flexed her muscles, and he was a

vast deal more than ready to weigh anchor in her harbor, again. "But without my Amanda I am already dead, so I had to risk it all for you."

"For us, I suspect." She inhaled a shaky breath. "And now I suppose we should return to the ballroom, as Papa awaits, but I would rather spend the night, here, with you."

"Perhaps." He shuffled the yards of silk to locate her bare bottom. With his hands at her hips, he held her firm as he thrust. "But there is no reason we cannot linger a tad longer."

And approximately ten minutes later, their clothes righted with precision, Mark escorted Amanda to the dining room, where the revelers had gathered for the celebratory meal. It was with no small measure of pride that he noted the flirty flush of her countenance had resurfaced with vigor and recalled what he had done to achieve such satisfactory results.

"At last." The marquess signaled them to band together at the head of the center table. "And your timing is perfect."

Mark could not agree more with his father-in-law's assessment, though their perspectives differed drastically. With his lady at his side, he bent and whispered, "Leave your window unlocked."

To wit Amanda cast him a coy smile and replied, "Stay on the center rungs of the trellis, as they have been reinforced."

Mark burst into laughter and then cleared his throat, as Hiram stood at attention and arched a brow.

"My lords, ladies, gentlemen, and honored friends and family." The marquess held high a crystal glass of champagne. "It is my distinct pleasure to share with you a bit of joy, the formal announcement of which shall appear in tomorrow's *Daily Universal Register*. Lady Eleanor and I ask you to join us in toasting the impending nuptials of our daughter, Lady Amanda Catherine Gascoigne-Lake to Captain Mark Andrew Douglas, of the Royal Navy and the recently commissioned HMS *Indomitable*."

∼

THE APRIL SHOWERS SUBSIDED, and the sun shone bright in a clear azure sky on Amanda's wedding day. Sitting at her vanity, because her escritoire had already been moved to Mark's ship, in preparation for an early May departure to patrol the Baltic, she penned an entry in the leather-bound journal, which accompanied the ancient badge that had, at first, caused her insurmountable distress.

To the bearer of this curious piece of jewelry,

Despite my initial skepticism, as manifested in the small dent at the edge, which occurred in a rare and uncharacteristic loss of feminine deportment for which I am profoundly remorseful, for a sennight I napped with the pin affixed to my morning dress, and visions of a naval captain's insignia haunted me without fail. Such dreams of my reported one true knight caused me great despair, because my beau carried the rank of lieutenant—or so I thought. Unbeknownst to me at the time, my sweetheart had made post. Let it be known that today, April 25, 1786, I shall marry my indomitable Mark Douglas, in keeping with the associated lore, captain of the vessel bearing the name reflecting the dominant trait of my future husband. Should nagging doubts plague your consciousness, in regard to the predictive nature as it pertains to the brooch, perhaps our affirmation, faithfully sworn and upheld, may allay your fears and gird your resolve.

Ego dilecto meo et dilectus meus mihi.

Respectfully Submitted,

Lady Amanda Gascoigne-Lake, soon-to-be-Mrs. Mark Douglas

"Excuse me, my lady." Ellie curtseyed. "But the marquess

requests your presence, as you must depart for the church, else you will be late."

"Coming, Ellie. Do not forget to air the red velvet, along with my pelisse, as I shall wear them when we depart for our honeymoon." Amanda stood and assessed her appearance in the long mirror. Flouting tradition, she had opted for another variation on the navy gown, *á la militaire*, complete with the requisite braiding on her long sleeves, because she wanted the world to know she was Mark's, in every way. "And can you make sure my sister receives the journal and accompanying pouch?"

"Yes, my lady." The maid sniffed and wiped a stray tear. "My, but you look lovely."

"Thank you, dear friend." At the door, she reminisced of the wonderful memories made in her chambers, most of which involved Mark's nightly forays through her window, since his return to London, and every seemingly unexceptionable piece of furniture that had served as means to assert his resourcefulness and virility, but she had not complained. In short, the man possessed Herculean vigor and a vivid imagination. With a smile and the burn of a blush, she skipped down the hall and descended the stairs.

In the foyer, Papa drew his timepiece from his pocket, and when he glanced at her, his expression softened. "Amanda, you are a vision, and I am not so sure Douglas deserves you. Daresay I could have secured a marquess or a duke for such beauty."

"Nonsense." She scoffed. "Why should I settle for less than my captain?"

"Well said, well said, my girl." Her father chuckled and extended his arm. "Shall we away, as your young man is a prompt sort, and we would not want him to think you have changed your mind? He has arrived at our doorstep precisely at nine for our daily jaunt through Hyde Park for the past fortnight."

"Yes, as I am quite anxious." Of course, she would never tell her father that Mark was so reliable because he had not far to travel. After riding her at dawn, he had only to climb down the trellis, exit the side gate, and stroll to the front door.

The journey by their town coach to Hanover Square and St. George's took only a few minutes. As the six-columned entrance came into view, her pulse beat a salvo of excitement. The equipage slowed to a halt, and Papa handed her to the sidewalk, where a crowd had gathered. Amanda waved at the well-wishers and then entered the church. As the pipe organ played Bach's "Prelude," in E-flat, she navigated the aisle to join her beloved at the altar, before the Archbishop.

At last, Mark, magnificent in his dress uniform, took her hands in his and pledged, "From this day forward you shall not walk alone. My heart will be your shelter, and my arms will be your home."

"By the power vested in me, I now pronounce you husband and wife." The Archbishop closed the Book of Common Prayer. "Captain Douglas, you may kiss your bride."

Although she knew not what to expect from her incorrigible sailor, given that more than half the *ton* and numerous naval officers had witnessed their vows, she poised for what should have been a mere formality. Instead, her exceedingly unpredictable spouse favored her with a mischievous grin, swooped, caught her in a bear hug, lifted her from her feet, and covered her mouth with his in a searing corporeal affirmation of their union, to spirited applause, hoots, and hollers.

Together, Amanda and Mark ran the gauntlet, which included an improvised archway of drawn swords by the commissioned crewmen from the *Indomitable*. At the bottom of the steps, a curricle bedecked with white crepe and clusters of spring flowers waited, and Mark deposited her to the box seat and then grabbed the reins.

"Darling, while I hesitate to correct your sense of direction, you just made a wrong turn." She clutched her bouquet of white roses. "And we do not want to be late for our reception."

"Married five minutes and already issuing orders, my officious little thing?" He laughed, settled an arm about her shoulders, and drew her close. "I have a surprise for you, my lady wife, and we cannot be late for our party, as it will not commence without us, because we are the guests of honor, but your father knows where we venture."

"He does?" Amanda's curiosity piqued, especially as they neared the Thames. "Mark, where are you taking me?"

To her frustration, he arched a brow in response.

When they passed the gate of the London Port, her question was answered, yet she understood not his motives. At St. Katharine Docks, she spied the *Indy*, and the mystery was solved, as she noted the festoon of evergreens hoisted to the main topgallant stay.

"Oh, Mark." Now she cried happy tears. "It is our wedding garland."

The centuries old custom of the British Navy announced the nuptials of a crewmember, and Amanda had seen many, as the daughter of an admiral. But that simple expression was far more arresting, as it was her garland.

"Your father had the *Indomitable* berthed here, for today, so we might enjoy it prior to our luncheon, as Great Dock is quite a drive, and we have little time." And then Mark produced a couple of leaves from his pocket. "For your keepsake, love."

"How thoughtful you are, my new husband." She giggled. "And I should endeavor to compose a suitable demonstration of gratitude."

"I am sure you will think of something, my Amanda." He

narrowed his stare. "You know my favorite boon, where you are concerned, and we must consummate our vows."

"Fear not, Captain." She batted her lashes and squeezed his thigh, which tensed at her touch. "As I have an idea."

"Then let us make our celebration, so we might begin the honeymoon." He turned the rig with expert horsemanship. "And I have another treat, of which I hope my bride approves."

"Ah, yes." He had refused to apprise her of their destination. "And do we travel this evening?"

"You will not get me that easy, sweetheart." He winked. "Although I am rather obliging, when it comes to you, but indulge me, as it is our wedding day."

"Because it is our wedding day, and I love you, I shall acquiesce." She clucked her tongue. "As it is, I have plans of my own."

"And are you certain you wish to sail with me?" He merged onto Park Lane. "If you have reconsidered, I will not be angry with you."

"Just try and cast off without me, Mark Douglas." In an instant, the pain of their long separation cast a chill over her heart, and she shivered. Had he second thoughts? "Do you not want me aboard your ship?"

"Of course, I do, as I would expend valuable energy, of which I have none to spare, worrying about your welfare. You are still too thin, darling." And then he frowned. "Yet it may kill me to depart London without you."

"Then do not leave me behind." And despite the fact they were in public, she snuggled to him and relaxed when he bent and kissed her temple. "As I will not survive another parting."

"Then we shall stay the course, my girl." He reined in at the entrance to her family residence. "Now, let us dine with your parents, because you will need all your strength for the night I have arranged."

"Is that a promise?" Oh, she hoped so, as she had her own scheme.

"You may depend upon it." After he descended, he turned and handed her to the gravel drive.

In the grand dining room, which spanned the length of the home from front to back, and opened to the ballroom, each table had been bedecked in crisp white linen trimmed in old gold and boasted a centerpiece of a huge cut-glass vase filled to overflow with white roses. The finest crystal, Sevres china, and silver had been placed with precision His Majesty would envy, and a quartet had been situated in the rear corner.

The meal passed in a blur, as Amanda was far too focused on her husband and his constant barrage of whispered seductions, all involving carnal pursuits of a questionable nature, his tongue, and her body—and she loved every minute of it. How difficult it had been to maintain a stoic expression the previous day, when her mother attempted to explain the mechanics of intercourse. Given Mark's tenacity and ingenuity, Amanda suspected she could teach Mama a thing or two.

"So, young Douglas, we are family, at last. Perhaps now you can give my big toe a rub." When cousin Helen diverted Mark's attention, as previously devised, Amanda winked at the eccentric spinster and slipped, unnoticed, from the party.

Once ensconced in her chambers, she doffed the navy gown and her chemise and then donned the red velvet, which her husband had specifically requested she wear on their honeymoon, just prior to her father's painful postponement of the betrothal. Standing at the long mirror, she smoothed the skirts. "Hurry, Ellie."

"I am tying as fast as I can, my lady." Ellie tugged hard on the laces. "But either the dress has grown, or you have shrunk, so I must pull extra tight to achieve the fit you seek."

With wicked intentions, Amanda eased down the bodice,

just shy of indecent, until she attained the desired display of décolletage, because she wanted Mark to fall at her feet. And then her husband had better perform, to her expectations, every single erotic undertaking he so carefully detailed during their wedding luncheon.

"There." Ellie stepped back to assess her handiwork and flinched. "Oh, my lady. I can see your bosom."

"That is the idea." Pleased with the outcome, Amanda smiled. "Now help me with the pelisse, because I need it fastened to my throat."

Approximately five minutes later, she descended the staircase, appropriately covered, where Mark waited in the foyer. "Are you ready to depart, Mrs. Douglas?"

"Oh, I love it when you call me that." She bounced with giddy anticipation. "And will you tell me where we journey?"

"No." He stole a quick kiss. "Because I look forward to your reaction."

Outside, as the evening sun sank low on the horizon, they ran amid a sea of family and friends. Again perched on the box seat of Mark's curricle, with the hood up, Amanda closed her eyes and tossed the bouquet. A cheer erupted, as some distant relation nabbed the bundle, and Mark flicked the reins.

From Park Lane, they turned north onto St. James's and then made a left on Piccadilly. At Berkley Street, they steered right and continued onto David Street, and sudden nervousness plagued her senses. At Grosvenor Street, Mark veered west, navigated halfway around the square, and then drove the horses left at Upper Brook Street, slowed, and drew rein before a resplendent mansion emblazoned with the number 24 in the masonry that framed the double-door entrance.

"What is this place?" Confused, Amanda hesitated before Mark lifted her from the curricle. And then he swept her into his arms and ascended the stairs.

"Our London residence." He claimed another kiss but lingered, ever so deliciously, until a stodgy character set wide the oak panels, and then Mark conveyed her across the threshold. "My gift to you, sweetheart, in commemoration of our new life, together. Furnish and decorate it, to your heart's content. Make it a home of which you are proud."

"Mark, it is wonderful." As her husband set her on her feet, she glanced from side to side and noted nary a stick of furniture, aside from the hall tree. "But it is empty. Are we to sleep on the floor?"

"Good evening, Captain Douglas." The butler bowed. "Everything has been arranged, per your specifications."

"Thank you, Hamilton." Mark ushered her forward. "And meet the mistress of the manor. This is Lady Amanda, my wife."

"Felicitations, your ladyship, on this most joyous day." Hamilton dipped his chin. "I am at your disposal. May I take your coat?"

"It is lovely to meet you, and I look forward to working with you, as we form our household and hire additional staff." She clutched the folds of her pelisse, as it was time to launch her strategy. "But I would rather my husband help me, just this once."

"Of course." With that, he smiled. "Will there be anything else, Captain Douglas?"

"No." Mark wrapped an arm about her waist. "You may take the remainder of the evening off, and return in the morning."

"As you wish." Again, Hamilton bowed and then disappeared down a side hall.

"To answer your question, I took the liberty of purchasing a few items to make our first night more relaxed." Mark made to unfasten the hook at her throat, but she covered his hand with hers, and he frowned. "But if my selections displease you, feel free to secure replacements."

"I assume you procured a bed?" She gave him her back, as she freed herself from the heavy outerwear.

"You are correct." He reached over her shoulders to grasp the lapels, and she wiggled from the sleeves. "Along with a large, cushioned chair and a comfy bench of serviceable height, because I would not bruise your knees as we did last Thursday."

"Ah, yes. The table in my sitting room was rather brutal, as it was not meant for such licentious purposes, but you compensated admirably for my discomfit." Her husband chuckled at her reminder of a particularly glorious coupling, while she counted to three and then faced him.

All display of humor ceased.

A palpable stillness invested the whole of his frame, after he dropped her pelisse to the floor, and his gaze fixed, as telltale sparks flickered in his blue eyes. Mark swallowed hard and compressed his lips. "You remembered."

"My most cherished Captain, I forget nothing where you are concerned." Boldness learned in the past few weeks under his voluptuous tutelage brought her to stand toe to toe with her husband, and she unbuttoned his coat and then splayed her fingers to his chest. "A promise was made, and a bargain struck, and I hold you to it, sir."

"My lady wife, I will oblige you." Through the velvet, he gently pinched a pert nipple, and then he cupped her breasts, as he rubbed his nose to hers in a sweet caress. Without warning, Mark scooped her into his arms and claimed her mouth in a searing response to her demand. And as he climbed the stairs, two at a time, he grinned and said, "Like fifty men, my Amanda."

EPILOGUE

April 25, 1813

As Amanda gazed at the staircase of her home on Upper Brook Street, countless happy memories played a festive mosaic. She recalled the first time Mark carried her into the elegant mansion and that unforgettable night. An image of Sabrina, the youngest Douglas girl, sliding down the bannister, much to her father's delight and her mother's chagrin, elicited a giggle. And then Amanda glanced into the drawing room where only last December Cara, the eldest daughter, revealed in spectacular if less than graceful fashion her love for Lance Prescott, an extended family member. Given the shock, poor Mark got foxed that evening.

"My lady, that was the final box of Lady Cara's belongings." Hamilton appeared misty-eyed. "Shall I dispatch the wagon?"

"Yes." Amanda wrapped her arms about herself. "It will be quiet without Cara and Sabrina in residence, yet I suppose we shall accustom ourselves to it, but not too soon, I hope. Is the Admiral at home?"

"Indeed, he is in his study, your ladyship." Hamilton waved to the driver and then shut the doors. "Will that be all?"

"Is everything in place?" She retrieved the wrapped parcel from the entry table and assessed her reflection in the oval mirror. A tad thicker about the waist, the only other distinguishing characteristic of her advancing age manifested in the salt sprinkled about her raven hair.

"I have made a reservation at a charming restaurant and purchased tickets for the theatre, and the staff is abound with excitement, your ladyship." He clasped his hands behind his back. "Again, I must express our profound gratitude for your ladyship's generosity. Dinner shall be conveyed to the sitting room, promptly at four-thirty, per your instructions, and we depart at five. Are you sure you do not wish me to assign just one maid to attend you?"

"I am positive, as the Admiral and I are quite capable of serving ourselves. And you are most welcome." For her plan to work for the singular occasion, she required absolute privacy. With that, Hamilton bowed, and she made for the study and her prey. After a short rap on the door, she entered. "Am I interrupting anything of importance?"

"My dear, as you are of paramount importance, you could never interrupt me." Sitting at his desk, Mark dropped his pen to the blotter. "I gather it is done?"

"Yes." She strolled to the window overlooking the sidewalk. "As we speak, the remains of Cara's personal items are en route to Raynesford House. And Hamilton informed me that Pitton discovered damage to the trellis, outside Cara's window."

"*What*?" Mark pounded his fist to the oak top. "I will kill Lance."

"Oh, no." The source of his ire dawned on Amanda, and she burst into laughter at the irony. "You will do no such thing, as he married her."

"Then I should damn well charge him for the repairs." And then he scratched his cheek and chuckled. "Like mother, like daughter, it would seem. And what have you there?"

"This?" She peered at the bundle, more than a little disappointed at his apparent detachment. "It is nothing. Just something I made for you, which I hope shall be of use."

"Now who do you think you are fooling, Amanda?" Mark arched a brow, stood, walked to the armoire, and retrieved a vast deal more than decent-sized gift, which he placed on the blotter.

"You remembered?" In that instant, her heart sang.

"How could I forget the most wonderful day of my life?" He wound a finger in a loop of the large lavender bow and then splayed his arms. "Happy twenty-seventh wedding anniversary, love."

"Oh, Mark." She charged into his waiting embrace. "Given Cara's wedding, Sabrina's pregnancy, the war, and the Brethren, I thought, perhaps, it might have slipped your mind."

"How often must I remind you that you are never far from my thoughts?" He patted her bottom. "Open your present."

"You, first." She bounced with unutterable elation and held her breath, as he tore the paper. "I pray it meets with your approval."

"Amanda, this is magnificent." He scrutinized the waistcoat she had constructed. "You have outdone yourself."

"Try it on for size." She spread the garment and picked a speck of lint from the material.

"Will you do the honors?" In mere seconds, he doffed his coat and waistcoat and then gave her his back. "A perfect fit, darling. Thank you."

And then he drew her miniature, with the now familiar dent, and her lace handkerchief from the old accouterment. After tucking the keepsakes in the pocket she had sewn expressly for the items, he winked.

"So you still carry them?" she inquired in a small voice.

"My talisman, which I should never be without." Mark shuffled his feet. "Your turn, darling."

"You need not have gone to any trouble, and whatever you purchased, I adore it, already." As years of ingrained deportment yielded to uncontrollable joy, Amanda yanked the ribbon, ripped the paper, jerked off the lid, and gasped. "Mark, it is just like the one I wore that day in the park, when you challenged that awful Clarendon to a duel."

"Not quite." He pulled the navy pelisse, *á la militaire*, from a bed of cotton and held it for her inspection. "This one bears a noticeable resemblance to the Admiralty, my Amanda."

"I do so love it when you call me that." As tears welled, she turned, and he draped the sumptuous coat over her shoulders. "And I remain *your* Amanda?"

"When have you existed as anything else?" He kissed the crest of her ear and then nuzzled her neck. "And you are as beautiful as the moment I first saw you, in the Northcote's ballroom."

"And despite your current rank, which is rather impressive, and the tufts of grey hair at your temples, you persist as my dashing Lieutenant Douglas." She sighed when he cupped her breasts.

With that, Mark sat in his chair, slapped his thighs, and flicked his fingers in unmistakable invitation. After returning the pelisse to the box, she stepped about his knees, descended to his lap, turned to face him, pushed the waistcoat wide, and slid her hands over his chest. In a flash, he claimed her mouth, and heat seared a path from their lips to her core, as he inched a hand beneath her skirts and rested his palm to her bare thigh.

When next they surfaced for air, she was breathless. "Have you much work to complete?"

"I should post a couple of orders today, but the rest can wait until tomorrow." He rubbed his nose to hers. "Why? Have you arranged a suitable ceremony? Are the girls coming for dinner?"

"No. I had thought we could retire early." She trailed her tongue along his jawline. "And we dine, alone, in our sitting room."

"But it is only past four." He hissed, when she suckled his lobe. "I am not hungry."

"Well that leaves me plenty of time to stimulate your appetite." She shifted, unhooked his breeches, and found his oh-so-dependable, rock-solid erection. "Although it appears I have already inspired you."

"Bloody hell, Amanda. What happened to my shy debutante who flushed beetroot red, from head to toe, every time I undressed her?" His muscles tensed, and he groaned. "Hold hard."

"I am holding hard." She worked his length, fast and rough, just as he liked it. "And you unleashed her twenty-seven years ago."

"Woman, you still make me tremble." He cleared his throat. "All right. Let me complete these communiqués—*blast*."

"What is wrong?" She continued her delicious assault, nipping his flesh, given the tide had turned in her favor.

"I tipped over the deuced inkwell." The smell of candle wax and a drumbeat signaled he had sealed the correspondence. "Made a mess of my blotter."

"The servants will see to it, in the morning." Now she straddled him. "I want you."

"Not here, as I prefer you in our bed, naked and spread beneath me." Mark caught her wrists and halted her play. "Upstairs—*now*."

"Do you recall the afternoon Sabrina walked in on us, as I pleasured you from beneath the desk, after I forgot to lock the door?" She eased from his lap and resituated her skirts. "I lingered so long, I thought I might never close my mouth again."

"Never hugged my blotter so tight." He guffawed and then grabbed his coat. "It took three attempts to contrive a noble errand to distract her, so I could get you off your knees."

"Yes, but as I recollect, I managed to fire your cannon." In fact, in that particular arena, Amanda always won. "And why are you buttoning your coat?"

"You truly need to ask?" His countenance was pure devil, as his animated Jolly Roger tented his breeches.

With the stalwart proof of Mark's arousal concealed, they exited the study, arm in arm.

"May I ask you something?"

"Of course."

"Do you regret that we never had a son?" A long hidden sorrow shot to the fore, as they had not discussed a particular tragic event during the subsequent tenure of their marriage. "Have you ever wondered about our firstborn? The one we lost?"

"My dear, in that regard, my only regret is I left you in Jamaica, with the Siddons." With a mighty frown, he pulled her close and resituated her in the crook of his shoulder, as they navigated the hall. "But I thought it the right tack, given your violent morning sickness, and you were so weak."

"You could not have predicted the horrid fever, which plagued the entire island, and everyone took ill." She rued ruining their special day, as they entered the foyer, and wondered whatever possessed her to broach the subject. "And I did not blame you. In fact, I fretted that you faulted me, after you destroyed the Siddons's library."

"What?" Mark came to an abrupt halt. "You believed me angry *with you*?"

Unable to form a response, Amanda bit her lip and nodded.

"Why did you not tell me?" He framed her chin and brought her gaze to his. "Is this how you have felt, all these years?"

She shrugged.

"My darling girl." The kiss he bestowed upon her was soft, sweet, and too brief. "You misunderstood my actions, which were born not of ire but of fear, as your condition was grave upon my return. I have faced death countless times in battle, but your demise I could not begin to fathom, as you are my life. And as for my heirs, I am exceedingly proud of our daughters, because my only preferences were that our babes were healthy and you survived."

"I am so glad to hear you say it." She sniffed, as a long-standing wound healed.

"I beg your pardon, Admiral." Hamilton bowed. "Your ladyship, everything is situated, as you directed. And on behalf of the entire staff, we wish you both a happy anniversary."

"Thank you, Hamilton." Mark retrieved two envelopes from his pocket. "Will you—"

"Please post this correspondence before you depart for the night." Amanda snatched the letters and passed them to the butler. "Also, when you speak with Pitton about the damaged trellis, tell him to bill the Marquess of Raynesford for the repairs. And that will be all."

"Yes, my lady." With a half smile, Hamilton made for the kitchen.

"My delectable wife, what manner of mischief are you about?" Mark loomed with hands on hips, and the mood had changed for the better, given his grin. "Out with it."

"I gave the household staff the rest of the day off, because I want you to myself." She grabbed him by the wrist and tugged him to the stairs. "Now take me to our chambers and make love to me like fifty men."

He narrowed his stare. "Officious little thing."

"Yes, but I am *your* officious little thing." She rocked on her heels.

"Damn straight." In a flash, her husband bent and swept her into his arms.

"Mark, be careful." She could not help but giggle. "You might injure yourself."

"Do you think me old?" he inquired, with an expression of horror.

"Oh, no." She nuzzled him. "Not you."

"So we are alone, tonight?" His husky tone all but heralded his licentious intent, and she thrilled to his response. At the landing, he turned left. "As we were, twenty-seven years ago?"

"Indeed." With a swift tug, she untied his stock and unfastened his shirt collar, as she sought contact with his heated flesh. Then she licked his ear. "Shall we re-enact our consummation?"

"An excellent suggestion, though I am unsure we can manage the myriad contortions we indulged that night, as I did everything but balance you on your head, but we shall endeavor to persevere." Mark carried her into their suite and kicked the door shut behind him. "As, my Amanda, I wager I can still make you scream."

A VERY BRETHREN CHRISTMAS

CHAPTER ONE

London
December 20, 1816

*I*t all started with an insult. A perfect storm of haphazard societal blunders provoked by an honest mistake, which resulted in unforgivable rudeness and a subsequent inexcusable slight, that helped Admiral Mark Douglas win the love of his life. Of course, he did not know it then, but the singular moment borne of ignorance would forever alter his destiny, in ways he could not have imagined at the time.

To her credit and his inexpressible good fortune, Lady Amanda, his cherished wife, had been blessed with a charitable spirit and a wicked sense of humor, because she took pity on a lowly sailor, pardoned his transgressions, and gifted her most precious possession—her heart. With his inimitable society miss at his side, he rose through the ranks of the Royal Navy with heretofore unheard-of haste, thanks to a lethal combination of his military prowess and her family connections.

The fortuitous turn of events led him to where he sat, in the chamber of Robert Dundas, second Viscount Melville and First

Lord of the Admiralty. Mark shifted his weight and peered at the world beyond the windows, as a light snow fell. In his mind he cursed, because he planned to depart the city for his country estate that afternoon, to arrive in time to celebrate Christmastide with his family, but the viscount's fickle behavior waylaid Mark's aim.

"This is ridiculous," whispered Admiral Frederick Maitland, one of Mark's oldest friends and confidants. "We have been here all morning. How long is he going to study the same bloody documents and charts?"

"Until he makes a decision regarding the open post." Just then, the viscount glanced in Mark's direction, opened and closed his mouth, and Mark held his breath, but Melville spoke naught. From his pocket, he pulled out his timepiece. "Hell and the Reaper, the hour grows late, and I am to leave for Kent for the holidays."

"Given the weather, that is not a good idea." Maitland arched a brow. "You had better wait until tomorrow morning, because the roads may be treacherous, and you could injure a horse or break a wheel, in the dark."

"It is a risk I am willing to take, or I may miss Christmastide." Mark tugged at his stock. "If that happens, Amanda will have my head or some other important part of my anatomy."

"That is why I never married." Maitland snickered. "Although your woman is quite handsome enough to tempt me. Alas, she only has eyes for you, which calls into question her sanity."

"Very funny." From his waistcoat pocket, he drew a miniature portrait. Framed in an oval gold encasement encrusted with tiny pearls and sapphires, the Cosway depicted Amanda's beauty but failed to capture her fiery spirit. That, alone, belonged to Mark. "And I consider Amanda's choice a sign of her uncommon intelligence."

"Well said, well said." Maitland winked and slumped over the armrest. "Now, if we could only escape this den of inane tedium before I lose my patience and run amok. Then I shall be arrested and discredited, and you will have to vouch for my character, that I might avoid permanent institutionalization in an asylum, where I will spend the rest of my days gazing at nothing, in silent reflection, and drooling."

"You know, I believe you missed your true calling." Mark snorted. "Because you could have been an actor on a stage."

Melville cleared his throat, and Mark and Maitland came alert.

"Gentlemen, each of you were summoned for an expressed purpose, and I thank you for your forbearance as I weighed my decision." The viscount closed a folder and rested his hands atop the blotter, and Mark sat at attention, hoping for a quick resolution and dismissal. "Before I announce the requisite promotions, I would have you know the process by which I came to certain conclusions."

Inwardly, Mark swore a blue streak.

For the next twenty or so minutes, Melville detailed various useless bits of procedure, none of which interested Mark. He crossed and uncrossed his feet, as he twiddled his thumbs. He folded and unfolded his arms. He shifted left and then right. He gritted his teeth against a groan of frustration, and just when he could take no more delays, the viscount met Mark's stare and smiled.

"Admiral Douglas, it is my pleasure to promote you to the position of First Sea Lord. As you know, that makes you military head of the Navy." In that moment, Mark could have swooned, as his ears rang, and the viscount said, "And Admiral Maitland, you are to be Second Sea Lord. My hearty congratulations, gentlemen." Melville stood, walked to a side table, lifted a crystal decanter, and poured three balloons of brandy. "Let us celebrate with a toast and, perhaps, dinner, as the hour is late, and I am famished."

"Bloody hell." Mark swore under his breath and clenched his fists, as he rose from his chair. "Er—thank you, sir." Of course, he could not decline the invitation. "It would be my honor."

"Then I shall offer a toast." Melville held high his glass, and Mark and Maitland followed suit. "To the Royal Navy and the Board of Admiralty. Long may we reign in service to the Crown."

"Hear, hear." Maitland glanced at Mark and arched a brow. "By all means, let us eat, else I may gnaw on my boot leather, because I am so hungry I could eat the arse end of a dead elephant."

"How appetizing." The viscount grimaced, set his glass on the desk, and retrieved his hat and coat from a wall peg. "Then let us away to Gunderson's, as I fancy their pork roast."

"Well this is a fine mess." At the rear, Mark huddled with Maitland, as they navigated a maze of halls. "I suppose I have no choice but to depart tomorrow. And what of you? Where will you spend the holidays?"

"Like you, I travel to my estate in Kent." Maitland shrugged into his greatcoat as they stepped outside, and a cold wind whispered and thrummed. "But I have no angry bride awaiting my arrival, so I am unhurried."

"Why don't you journey with me?" Mark signaled his coachman. "I would enjoy your company, and Amanda will only be vexed if I am late for Christmastide, but I submit she will forgive me when she hears of my promotion."

"If it is not too much trouble." As usual, Maitland thrust two fingers into his mouth and gave vent to an earsplitting whistle. "And Melville could not have chosen a better man for First Sea Lord, my lord."

"The title is used only when I act in official capacity, and I will thank you to remember that, because I was not to the manor born." Mark shook his head and frowned at the grey clouds and now heavy snowfall. "Do me a favor. Be at my home at dawn, because I would depart, posthaste."

~

DESPITE THE RELATIVELY EARLY HOUR, the foyer posited a dark cavern, as Lady Amanda Douglas lit a candle and peered out the window. To her dismay, the world beyond the glass manifested a winter wonderland, as snow blanketed the earth beneath an angry sky. Normally, she would pass the time abed, with her husband, but Mark had yet to come home, and she fretted for his safety, given he was overdue to arrive.

Shivering, she pulled her Norwich shawl over her shoulders and lamented the absence of her naval man, because Mark possessed a particular flair for keeping her warm, and she longed for his strong embrace and soul-stirring kisses. Never should she have let him talk her into departing for Kent without him, a fortnight ago, because they always traveled together. But their youngest, Horatio, waned in town. Much like his father, he preferred the country, and Mark fretted for his son's health. However, in the future, she would remain at Mark's side. On the entry table, she spied an envelope and a small box addressed to her, and she snatched both items.

"Good morning, my lady." Hamilton, the butler, bowed. "Breakfast is served in the back parlor, per your wishes. And I had Cook prepare a pot of the tea you favor so much, as we received a delivery yesterday."

"Hamilton, when did this letter and parcel arrive?" she asked, as she tore open the note and unfolded the parchment. "And my thanks, because you are attentive, as always."

"Before dawn, my lady." Hamilton scrutinized a misplaced

vase of hothouse roses, a gift from Mark, which was delivered the previous day, and adjusted the blooms. "Given it was not marked as urgent, and the messenger did not indicate it was an emergency, I did not think it wise to disturb you."

"But it could be important, as we are expecting the entire family for Christmastide." Franked in London, the missive bore telltale script, and her fingers shook. "Oh, it is from the Admiral."

December 17, 1816

My darling Amanda,

I hope this note finds you well, even as I am grievously wounded by our continued separation and pining for your sweet face, which haunts me every moment we are apart. While I planned to depart London on the eighteenth, and gave you my word I would do so, I am delayed by order of the First Lord of the Admiralty, Viscount Melville, and duty calls, my lady. Thus, I shall quit the city on the twentieth, after the morning meeting. Please, know that this news hurts me far more than it does you, as I am tormented by your absence in our bed, which is so very cold without your loving and oh-so accommodating presence.

When we are reunited, sooner than later, if I am lucky, I shall endeavor to express the depth of my suffering—like fifty men, my Amanda. By now, you know what that means, and you had better brace yourself, because I am coming for you, my girl. Until that happy time, I offer a modest token, which harkens a resemblance to your eyes but pales in comparison to your beauty, in the expressed hope that you might take pity on a poor seaman and wear it, and it alone, for my delectation, when I am again sheltered in your unyielding embrace.

All my love,
Your Mark

"Felicitous tidings, I pray?" The butler, whose service to the family began on Mark and Amanda's wedding day, stretched tall and shuffled his feet. "Is the Admiral well, my lady?"

"You could say that, and the Admiral is in fine fettle." Married thirty years, and the man could still compose a *billet-doux* that gave her gooseflesh. With a smile, she resolved to add his latest composition to her rather impressive collection, which dated to their courtship. "And according to his message, he should have left London sometime today, when I had anticipated he would be home." Biting her lip in anticipation, as her thoughts ran wild, given Mark's salacious habits, which she adored, she tore the brown paper from the box and lifted the lid. Inside, resting on a bed of pristine cotton, sat a stunning necklace of gold, with diamonds and sapphires. "Oh, Mark."

Although she wore a simple morning dress of blue muslin, she unhooked the clasp and fastened the precious bauble about her neck, to honor her husband. When he returned, she would fulfill his request, as well as a few unspoken others, because his desires were many, and she would enjoy every minute of the seduction.

"My lady, we have visitors." Hamilton narrowed his stare and stood at the ready. "Based on the various equipages, I suspect it is Lady Cara, Lady Sabrina, and perhaps Sir Ross and Lady Elaine. And I do not recognize the coat of arms on the last rig."

"Upon my word, but they are early, and it appears that coach carries my nephew George, when he never responded to my invitation." Amanda clapped twice in mild panic. "Please, ensure their rooms are prepared, and I will greet our guests. Also, have the table set in the dining room, and we will take breakfast there, as I suppose they will be hungry." From the hall tree, she grabbed her wool pelisse. "You had better warn Cook, because two eggs and a slice of toast will not feed seven additional adults and their small army of children."

CHAPTER TWO

December 21, 1816

A violent jostle wrenched Mark from a naughty dream involving his delectable wife, specifically her sumptuous bosom, amid which he loved to bury his face, and a healthy portion of warm cherry compote, which he preferred to lick from her nipples. No matter how much time passed, it always surprised him that his desire for his lady never faded. And it was not that his love had diminished, because she was his life. But, despite the fact that she routinely filled his bed, he could not get enough of her.

Rubbing his eyes, he sat upright in the squabs and pulled a lace-edged handkerchief from his waistcoat pocket, which Amanda gave him when he dueled with that clown Clarendon to restore her honor. After inhaling the subtle scent of jasmine, which she favored, he invoked a treasured image of his wife. A jarring noise tore him from his licentious reverie and he frowned at Frederick, who rattled the roof of the coach. With a yawn, he kicked his friend's boot and groaned as Frederick stirred.

"Did I disturb you?" Maitland wrinkled his nose and sniffled. "Was I snoring?"

"Did you disturb me, and were you snoring? Oh, no." Mark rolled his eyes. "Brother, you were not calling just one hog. You summoned an entire passel. Really, it is a blessing you never married, else your wife would permanently banish you to your study."

"But I am not so encumbered, so I am free to make as much noise as I please." For a ghost of an instant, a hint of sadness invested Frederick's expression, but he quickly recovered his wit. "And I follow my own orders, not those of an angry bride."

"You know, that reminds me of something." Mark snapped his fingers. "Were you not engaged to a distant cousin or some such?"

"A momentary lapse of sanity." Frederick winced and peered out the window. "The snow is getting worse."

"As long as the lanes are navigable, and we can continue our journey, the weather concerns me not." Although Mark would have much preferred to snuggle beneath the covers with Amanda. Again, he assessed his friend and noted the change in his appearance. Equal in height, they were often mistaken for kin in their prime, but now Frederick sported a gotch-gut and a double chin. "So tell me why you never took a wife, because you are a good man, and do not deflect the question."

"I suppose you might say that war got in the way." Frederick scratched his cheek. "And we are not all for the altar. Some of us prefer the easy friendships and superficial entanglements of a skilled courtesan."

"But you did not always sing that tune." Mark folded his arms. "As I recall, on a night we shared the watch aboard the *Seahorse*, when we were naught but midshipmen on patrol in the Baltic, you lamented the long separation from your special lady. What was her name? Anne? Alice?"

"Abigail." Frederick pointed for emphasis. "And I was young and foolish then. Not so, anymore."

"I will grant you the young part," Mark replied with a chortle. "As to the rest—"

Another forceful jolt thrust them both to the floor, and then the entire rig pitched and heaved, as the team screamed in protest.

"Bloody hell." They swerved, and Frederick clung to the bench. "Hold hard, Mark, because I think we are going to founder."

In that moment, Mark clutched the edge of his seat, as an anchor, and hunched on the floor, in the event they rolled. In silence, he uttered a prayer and pictured his family, as his life flashed before his eyes.

Amanda shimmered as an ethereal creature, gowned in indigo velvet, with her black hair piled in curls atop her head, as he first saw her in the Northcote's ballroom, more than thirty years ago. Cara and Sabrina, his daughters, smiled and curtseyed. And then there was Horatio, his son named for his longtime commander Vice Admiral Nelson.

Gritting his teeth, he rudely plunged into the present. The coach listed sharply, lurched upright with an unholy crack, and keeled to the left, and he feared they might topple, but the driver brought them safely to a halt.

"Well, that was close." As he gathered his wits, he crawled to the squabs and settled his coat. Then he noted the pronounced droop of the rig. "But I wager we broke a wheel. Still, ours is not to worry, given I had a spare tied with our trunks."

As if on cue, the coachman opened the door.

"Admiral Douglas, my apologies, sir." He doffed his hat. "Despite my best efforts to temper our speed, due to the poor road conditions, it appears we broke the axle, and we cannot proceed at this time."

"Please, tell me you are joking." Mark jumped from the coach and surveyed the damage. Squatting, he frowned. "And we lost a rear wheel and several spokes from another." Standing, he shook his head. "Well, this is a fine mess. Now we will never make it home in time for Christmastide, and Amanda may never forgive me."

"Belay that." Frederick slid on the ice and splayed his arms for balance. "Why don't we take a couple of horses and ride to the nearest town for assistance? We can leave your man here in the event someone comes along."

"That would be an excellent suggestion, were it not for the fact that the Shires are draft horses and not trained for riding, thus you may break your neck if you attempt to mount one." Mark huffed in frustration, glanced from side to side, and consulted his pocket watch. Since they ventured forth that morning, and exited London's environs via the toll gate more than four hours ago, they had spied nary a soul on the turnpike, so it seemed unlikely that aid would arrive anytime soon. "Given my experience based on countless trips home, I know there is a town nearby. It is Dartford, I believe."

"Are you suggesting we continue on foot?" Frederick asked in a sharp tone. "You must be out of your mind, because we will freeze to death before we make it anywhere."

"Then you had better don your greatcoat, hat, and gloves." Mark collected his warm outerwear. "Because we are walking."

∼

IN THE STUDY, Amanda tallied her ledger and savored the quiet calm of her husband's sanctuary. Somewhere in the house, a burst of laughter startled her, and her hand shook, as she almost knocked over the inkwell. "Blast." She covered her mouth, as if someone might have witnessed her momentary breach in polite decorum. "*Oh.*"

Then she laughed at herself, because she had engaged in far more questionable behavior in that room, which had seen almost as much action as the four-poster she shared with her seaman. How many times had Mark made a mess of the blotter, when she initiated various trysts at his desk? She smiled. Too many to count, a fact of which she was rather proud. "My darling, how I miss you."

After closing the journal, she pushed back the chair and stood. At the front window, she searched the graveled drive for any sign of Mark and almost shrieked with excitement when she noted an approaching coach. But then she realized there were six more equipages in the small caravan, and her sails deflated.

With a stiff upper lip to mask her disappointment, she strolled into the hall. In the foyer, she checked her appearance in the wall mirror and smoothed a few stray tendrils. Nabbing her pelisse, she peered over her shoulder, just as Hamilton approached.

"It appears the Duke and Duchess of Rylan, the Duke and Duchess of Weston, the Earl and Countess of Lockwood, and Captain Collingwood and Lady Alex, along with their children, are just arrived." And that meant she would know little peace, because the ducal duo manifested the heart and soul of the Brethren of the Coast, the famed Nautionnier Knights descended from the Order of the Knights Templar, the warriors of the Crusades. When Blake and Damian were in residence, mayhem ensued, and she would have it no other way. "Did you remember to house them as far apart as possible, because I would not have a repeat of our last family gathering?"

"Yes, my lady." The butler's expression implied even the household staff recalled the unusual contest between the fiercely competitive friends, more like brothers, wherein they attempted to determine which husband could better satisfy his bride, based on the effuse exultation articulated mid-coitus, and no one got any sleep for days. After summoning the footmen, he set wide the double doors. "We are ready, and I have refreshments set up in the drawing room."

"Hamilton, I know not why I question you, when you are always reliable." Amanda descended the entrance stairs, as an army of liveried footman assisted her guests. "Blake and Lenore, it is wonderful to see you."

"Lady Amanda, we wish you a Happy Christmas." Blake kissed her cheek. "And we would share our felicitous news. Lenore is expecting our second child."

"I am not surprised, and I daresay your mother is thrilled." Of course, that was a predictable outcome of the ducal rivalry, she laughed. "Do come inside and warm yourself by the fire." To Lenore, Amanda said, "And there is plenty of hot tea and scones. But where is Sarah?"

"Thank you, Lady Amanda." Lenore dipped her chin.

"Mama travels with Dirk's mother and Dirk and Rebecca." Blake slipped an arm about Lenore's shoulders and nuzzled her temple. "They were waiting on Dalton and Daphne, and their children, in Maidstone, that they might continue the journey together."

Just then, Damian and Lucilla neared.

"Lady Amanda, we bid you Happy Christmas." Damian rested a palm to Lucilla's belly and grinned. "And we impart the joyous news of my impending heir."

"*Damian.*" Lucy pouted. "I thought we were going to delay until dinner to share our good fortune."

"Forgive me, sweetheart." He kissed her forehead. "But I could not wait."

"You, too?" Puffing his chest, Blake smirked. "Lenore and I expect our second child."

"Indeed." Damian thrust his chin. "I should have known you could not do anything without me, so I suppose you have me to thank."

"Now, see here—"

"Blake, if you are going to spend the holiday arguing with Damian, you may share his room." Lenore reached for and grasped Lucy's hand. "And my sister can bunk with me."

"I concur." Lucy stomped a foot. "And my darling Damian, if you crow about that audacious wager one more time, you may sleep in the stables, because I am tired of hearing about it. You did not get me with child on your own, because I had something to do with it, too."

"Now, sweetheart, don't be angry with me, as I am uncontrollably excited about the addition to our family." Damian whispered in her ear, and she blushed. Amanda could only imagine what he said. "What say we retire to our accommodation for a hot bath?"

"That sounds lovely." When Lucy turned toward the house, Damian glanced at his chief antagonist and stuck out his tongue, to wit Blake responded in kind.

"Stop it." Lenore swatted at Blake. "Whatever am I to do with you?"

"I am only too happy to offer suggestions." Blake waggled his brows. "Let us go inside before you catch a cold."

Shaking her head, Amanda laughed and greeted her other guests. "Jason and Alex, I am so relieved you made it."

"As are we." Jason gazed heavenward. "The roads were treacherous, and it was dreadfully slow going. Has the Admiral arrived from London?"

"Not yet, but I expect him at any moment." Given Jason's ominous warning, she shivered but not from the cold. "Please, go inside and get settled." To Trevor and Caroline, she waved a greeting, while they helped their nanny corral their five children.

Once everyone entered the residence, and a small compliment of nannies rustled the next generation of Brethren upstairs, Amanda loomed in the doorway, staring up the drive.

"Is everything all right, my lady?" As she retreated into the foyer, the butler closed the oak panels and set the bolt.

"I am not sure." Rubbing the back of her neck, she mulled the empty peg where Mark hung his outwear, and gooseflesh covered her from top to toe. For some reason she could not explain, she struggled with a dark sense of foreboding. Something was wrong, and no one would convince her otherwise. "Station a footman at the door, until the Admiral arrives, and wake me, no matter the hour."

CHAPTER THREE

December 22, 1816

 *H*uddled beneath the warm covers, Mark came awake and smiled smugly, given the soft body that hugged him from behind. Ah, his Amanda always snuggled close in the winter months. Then again, she sought his attention year-round, especially in their bed, and that was fine with him. Resolved to give her what she wanted, he reached down and caressed what seemed to be a rather large thigh.

 Telltale snoring cut through the delicious fantasy, and he recalled his current predicament in vivid detail. With a violent flinch, he fell off the mattress and connected rudely with the floor.

 "Frederick, what in bloody hell are you doing?" Standing, Mark raked his fingers through his hair and then kicked the frame. "Wake up, man."

 "Hmm?" Frederick snuffled and farted, and Mark almost vomited. "What is it?"

 "Er, it is nothing." When he realized his friend had no idea what happened, Mark cleared his throat and grabbed his boots.

"But I want to get an early start, and we have yet to find a way home, so you had better get moving."

"All right." Sitting upright, Frederick stretched his arms overhead and yawned. "You know, I did not think I could rest, given the inn had only one room available, with a single bed, due to the weather and the holidays, but I slept surprisingly well."

"Indeed, you did." Mark shrugged into his waistcoat and tucked Amanda's portrait miniature, along with her lace-edged handkerchief, in the pocket she sewed into the garment for just that purpose. "In fact, you never stirred when the coachman knocked to apprise me of his arrival and the condition of the rig."

"After that long walk in the frigid storm, and the hot meal, I was more than ready to collapse." Frederick scooted from the mattress, discovered one sock missing, and searched among the covers. "Where do you get your stamina, given we are the same age? And what news from the coachman?"

"My wife." At the washstand, Mark cleaned his teeth and scrubbed his face. "As for the coach, not good, I am afraid. The axle is broken clean in two, and most of the local businesses are closed. The stableman I hired managed to retrieve our trunks and the horses, and he brought my driver into town. Clegg will remain in Dartford until the coach is repaired and then continue to Faversham."

"Where does that leave us?" Frederick tied his cravat in a less than elegant mathematical. "I am not opposed to staying here, especially if I can procure my own accommodation, because no one awaits my arrival."

"That is not an option, and the innkeeper made it clear this room was available for only one night, given it is already reserved for the holiday." In the long mirror, Mark scrutinized his neck cloth. "Now, I will go downstairs, settle our account, and meet you in the dining room, where we shall break our fast, so do not delay."

With that, he crossed the room, opened the door, and strode into the hallway. In the reception area, he approached the desk and flagged the innkeeper.

"Good morning, Admiral Douglas." The innkeeper smiled. "I hope you passed a pleasant night."

"I did, thank you." Excepting the rude awakening that still gave Mark a twinge of nausea. "Have you had any luck securing a hack that might convey me to Faversham?"

"I checked with every possible stable, and either all coaches are already let, or the proprietors refuse to rent them, owing to the poor road conditions, which you must understand, in light of your accident."

"Of course." Mark sighed, because it seemed all was lost, and he would not be home for Christmastide. "Thank you, Mr. Armbruster."

Dispirited, Mark turned just as his coachman walked into the foyer.

"Admiral, sir, I was just coming to find you." Clegg doffed his hat and nodded once. "I may have found you passage to Rochester."

"Rochester?" Mark shifted his weight. "But what good will that do me?"

"It gets you halfway to Faversham, sir." Averting his gaze, Clegg shuffled his feet. "Perhaps, you can find another means of travel from there."

"You are right." Mark tamped his frustration, because Rochester was but a couple of hours from Faversham, by coach. "Tell me of your plan."

"There is a stablemaster in need of riders to help him deliver a set of mares to a business in Rochester." Clegg compressed his lips. "He will pay you, sir, and you must leave in one hour."

"Then I haven't a moment to spare." Mark signaled Frederick, as he descended the stairs. "Come and let us eat."

"Did you find us a way home?" Frederick turned up his nose, as they sought an empty table. "Over by the window there is a place."

"When is the last time you rode a horse?" Mark braced for the response.

"About five years ago, as I am a sea captain, not a cavalryman." Frederick pulled out a chair and sat. "Why do you ask?" He glanced at Mark, then Clegg, and then back at Mark. "Whatever you have arranged, I get a peculiar inkling I am not going to like it."

"Well, this could be interesting." Mark draped a napkin in his lap. "And I have a feeling you are going to hate it."

∽

FROM THE DRAWING ROOM WINDOW, Amanda stood as sentry, awaiting Mark's return. Based on his letter, she expected his arrival by the previous evening, at the latest. It was for that reason she had not slept much, and she grew more concerned by the hour.

"Mama, please, do not worry." From behind, Cara hugged Amanda. "Papa will be home soon, and he will be vexed when he learns how you fretted for him."

"It is understandable that he would be delayed," Sabrina stated with an expression of sympathy. Heavily pregnant, she rested on a *chaise*. "The roads were positively dreadful, and—"

"Clegg is the finest coachman in all of England." Cara huffed a breath. "If anyone can navigate the turnpike, in any condition, he can, is that not right, sister?"

"*Oh*—yes, of course." Sabrina sputtered and swiped a piece

of shortbread from the tea trolley. "That is precisely what I meant to say."

"Indeed, we arrived a day after Sabrina and Cara, and the lanes were a vast deal more than manageable." Alex poured a cup of tea and reclined in a Hepplewhite chair. "Will you not come and sit with us?"

"I appreciate what you are trying to do." Wringing her fingers, Amanda joined Elaine on the sofa. "But Jason said the roads were treacherous."

"The man has no sense." Alex waved dismissively but did not convince Amanda. "Besides, he is rather occupied with more important business, because he indulges in a new wager."

"Not another one." Caroline rolled her eyes. "Really, Blake and Damian just finished their test of wills, with Lenore and Lucy offering evidence to that effect. What is it now?"

"Actually, I planted the suggestion in my husband's ear, because I want another babe." Cara strolled to the hearth and warmed her hands. "So Lance and Jason are competing to see which of them can conceive a new addition with their respective wives."

A chorus of giggles erupted, and Amanda relaxed, as she enjoyed the company.

"But Alex is already pregnant," Sabrina blurted. Then she quickly covered her mouth. "Uh-oh."

"*Sabrina*, you promised you would not tell anyone." Alex folded her arms. "And I am not entirely certain of my condition, so I would thank you to keep my secret."

"I do not understand." Eileen, Sir Ross's younger sister and new member of the family, tapped a finger to her chin and furrowed her brow. "If the wager is to conceive first, then Captain Collingwood is done, is he not?"

"My dear Eileen, you know that, and I know that, but what my husband does not know will not hurt him." With a cat-that-ate-the-canary grin, Alex hugged a pillow to her belly. "Besides, I am enjoying this contest, and I would not dare interfere in his manly pursuits, because it inspires his poetry."

"Well said, Alex." Cara raised her teacup in toast, and Amanda could not help but laugh, because Jason's original, ribald compositions were the stuff of legend in the Brethren circles. "Likewise, I am quite enamored of Lance's attentiveness and dedication to the cause. Who am I to disillusion him?"

Another chorus of mirth filled the room, but Amanda could not forget Mark. As the Brethren wives discussed the benefits of married life, she realized that, in her preoccupation with her husband's absence, she neglected Eileen, who seemed a tad out of sorts, given it was her first Christmastide with the large, extended family.

"Eileen, I wonder if you might assist me in a minor task." Amanda stood and flicked her fingers. "If it is not too much trouble."

"It would be my honor, Lady Amanda." Eileen stood and deposited her cup on the trolley. "How can I be of use?"

"Let us adjourn to the library, given the men congregate in Mark's study, and I will explain what I need." As they walked into the hall, Amanda signaled Hamilton. "How are the preparations coming for Stir-Up Day?"

"We are almost ready, my lady." The butler bowed. "Perhaps, we can gather in the kitchen, in half an hour?"

"Perfect. That will be all, Hamilton." Amanda steered Eileen toward the back of the house. "Every year, when we observe the Christmastide tradition, I provide a quick summation of the holiday custom, because there are those among us who never took part in Stir-Up Day."

"Myself included." Eileen followed in Amanda's wake, as they navigated the massive collection of books. "Upon my word, but this library is magnificent."

"It is my husband's favorite place, and he spends hours in here, when he is in residence." How she pined for her man, especially when she spied the two-seater bench, upon which her husband often seduced her. "I believe there is a book—"

"Who goes there?" George queried in a tone to which she took great exception.

"I beg your pardon?" Amanda stopped and rested fists to hips. "Who dares question my presence in my home?"

"Aunt Amanda, my apologies." George shifted, when she arched a brow. "And to Miss Logan, if I offended her."

"No offense taken, Viscount Huntingdon." To Amanda's surprise, Eileen curtseyed.

"My dear, we are family here. We do not stand on formalities, thus we do not use titles within these walls." On a table, Amanda located the reference she sought. "Ah, here it is."

"Do you read, Miss Logan?" George rocked on his heels, and Amanda viewed him in a new light, as he interacted with Eileen.

"Of course." Eileen narrowed her stare. "Do you?"

"That is some cheek, Miss Logan." George stretched tall.

"Unlike yourself." She half-smiled. "Why, you evidence the whole of polite society, from A to B, Viscount Huntingdon."

"Impossible woman." George bared his teeth. "If you were my wife, I would poison your tea."

"Viscount Huntingdon, if you were my husband, I would drink it." Then Eileen turned to Amanda. "But I ignore my hostess, when you asked for my aid."

Before Amanda could reply, her nephew stepped to the fore. "What does my aunt require?"

"A brief review of the history of Stir-Up Day, if you can manage it." She flipped to the requisite page. "But if you intend to help, then you had better comport yourself as I would expect of a nobleman." She wagged a finger. "Do not make me write your mother."

"Yes, Aunt Amanda." From her escritoire, George gathered a pen, an inkwell, and some stationary.

When the two put their heads together, Amanda backed from the area, but she monitored their interactions, as they continued to hurls insults, neither sportive nor serious. But it was when Eileen began to write that George admired her and smiled. They would bear watching.

CHAPTER FOUR

December 23, 1816

A braying ass startled Mark awake, and he lurched upright in a bed of hay, his meager accommodation when he could secure no room in town. Rubbing the small of his back, he winced, given the previous day's ride in driving snow brought him low. But it also saw him to Rochester and that much closer to home and his Amanda.

In the next stall, telltale snoring left him shaking his head. While he hated to wake his friend, because Frederick groused the entire journey to Rochester, Mark had to keep moving.

Wincing, he stood and rubbed his abused arse. With a newfound respect for the cavalry, he stumbled his way outside. To his dismay, the snow seemed to have intensified overnight.

"Good morning, Admiral Douglas." Cuthbert, the stablemaster, waved a greeting. "I brought you and Admiral Maitland something to eat. It is not much, just some bread and fresh milk, but you are welcome to it."

"I am grateful, Cuthbert." Mark accepted the pitcher and the basket. "Any developments in regards to a hack that might deliver me to Faversham?"

"Sorry, sir." Cuthbert shrugged. "I suppose it is the weather that is keeping everyone at home. There are no horses for rent, and I had word that even the stage and mail coaches have stopped until the storm passes."

"Bloody hell." Disappointed, Mark searched his mind for any solution. Then a vision of his Amanda flashed before him, as she paced before the drawing room window, and he shook himself alert. "Is there anything else you might think of, however far-fetched, that might see me safely to my family? Please, I am desperate. There is no price I would not pay."

"Sir, money is not the issue—wait a minute." Cuthbert snapped his fingers. "My wife's cousin operates a chicken farm a few miles outside town. He makes regular trips to Faversham, and I wager he would give you a ride if I asked him."

"Would you?" Then and there, Mark promised to return and compensate the young couple, because they had shown him immeasurable kindness. "I would be in your debt."

"Nonsense, sir." The stablemaster shoved his hands into the pockets of his threadbare coat. "I was wondering if I might ask a question."

"Of course." Mark nodded. "What is it you wish to know?"

"Did you know Nelson?" Cuthbert inquired.

"Indeed." Mark smiled. "I served as his first lieutenant, aboard the *Boreas*, and I was honored to count him a friend."

"What was he like?"

"Fierce in combat and in life." Mark chuckled. "He was a seaman's seaman, always leading from the front instead of the rear. But I appreciated his capacity for judging and advancing men based on their ability and merit, as opposed to their political connections, given I was but the second son of a viscount with little to recommend me except my tenacity and work ethic."

"You probably have fascinating tales to tell, and I would dearly love to hear them, but I should saddle the horses and prepare the sleigh, if we are to set off." The stablemaster turned but then paused and peered over his shoulder. "The only problem we have is the sleigh has but two seats."

"Then I shall remain here." Lingering in Mark's wake, Frederick frowned. "Because I am not sitting in your lap."

"Well, sir, based on your weight, I would suggest Admiral Douglas sit in your lap." Cuthbert snickered and then checked his stance. "But that is your choice. Eat your breakfast, while I make ready the sleigh, and I will be right back."

"All right." Mark strode past Frederick. "Let us adjourn to the stable, where is it warm."

"No." Despite his professed refusal, Frederick retraced Mark's steps. "I will not do it."

"There is fresh milk and bread." In the stable, Mark squatted and pulled a healthy portion from the loaf. "And we have no choice."

"*You* have no choice." Frederick grunted as he plopped to the ground. "I can do whatever I please, because no one waits for me." After shoving a huge piece of bread into his mouth, he slumped his shoulders. "First I shared your bed. Then you dragged me halfway across Kent on a horse, and my arse may never be the same again. Now I am to ride to God knows where in a sleigh with you in my lap? Brother, I love you, but that is where I draw the line."

"You will do no such thing, because you are coming with me, and if memory serves we did much worse as midshipmen." Mark gulped down the milk and handed the pitcher to Frederick. "Finish your meal, because we must away."

"Why am I doing this?" He averted his stare. "I could have stayed in London."

"And been all alone." Outside, bells jingled, and Mark scrambled to his feet. "Come, as I believe it is time to depart."

Groaning, Frederick stood and dusted off his breeches. "Something tells me I will live to regret this."

"Not at all." Then Mark extended a hand. "I would have your word as a gentleman that you will never breathe a word of this again, as long as you live."

"You think I want anyone to know I journeyed with you in my lap?" Frederick accepted the gesture, sealing the pact. "Well, let us have done with it."

∼

It was not quite a minute after Amanda hung the kissing bough in the entry to the drawing room that the Brethren husbands lined up their wives to take turns claiming their boon. Grateful for the distraction, she tried not to obsess over Mark's continued absence, telling herself he was delayed by some unforeseen assignment and would soon arrive.

"Are they always like that?" Eileen loomed to the right and laughed, just as Sir Ross cornered Elaine. "Because I have never witnessed such displays of affection, and that goes double for my brother."

"Why, Miss Logan, don't you know that all Brethren marry for love?" To Amanda's surprise, George engaged Eileen in more verbal fencing, and she pretended not to notice that they still employed formal addresses, which she suspected they did to aggravate each other. "Or do you not believe in such fancies?"

"I believe in many things." Eileen turned to face him. "None of which would interest you."

"Is that so?" George stepped in her direction, and Eileen retreated, and Amanda immediately guessed his aim. "Just how do you know what does or does not interest me?"

"Must I explain it to you?" Again, George encroached, and again Eileen withdrew, bringing her ever closer to the bough. "In order to care, you must first have a heart."

"Big words for a little lady." He neared, and Eileen gave ground. A warning danced on the tip of Amanda's tongue, but she kept silent. "Do you think me dim-witted?"

"Oh, no." She smiled far too sweetly. "You are as sharp as a marble, Viscount Huntingdon."

"Yet smart enough to corral you." Gloating, he pointed to the kissing bough, which now dangled above Eileen's head. "Well, Miss Logan? You know the lore. If you refuse me, you will not marry in the next year."

"George." Amanda advanced, just as Sir Ross took note of the situation.

"Huntingdon, do not accost Eileen, else I will box your ears." The venerable head of the Counterintelligence Corps glowered. "I did not bring my sister to entertain you."

"It is all right, brother." Eileen squared her shoulders and gained newfound respect from Amanda. "Yes, I know the lore, Viscount Huntingdon, and I am not concerned, because I have no intention of marrying anyone, ever. But I will satisfy you, not because I have any desire to join society but because I am a proud provincial."

Perched on tiptoes, she made to kiss George's cheek, in full view of the family. At the last moment, he shifted, and their lips met for the briefest instant. Eileen drew back as if he struck her, and she touched her fingertips to her mouth. Then she ran across the foyer and upstairs.

"*Eileen.*" When George would have given chase, Amanda stayed him, and it did not escape her notice that he at last dropped the formalities.

"You arrogant ass." Ross followed in his sister's wake, with Elaine not far behind. "She has never been kissed."

"The study—now." Amanda dragged her errant nephew by the arm and rued Mark's absence, because upbraiding men in the family was his duty, not hers.

"Aunt Amanda, I apologize." At a side table, George poured a glass of brandy, and his hands shook. "I never meant to frighten her."

"But you did, in my home." At the hearth, she paced to relieve the anger simmering just below the surface. "Eileen is family, and I will not have you enacting a seduction under my roof. Although she is no debutante, she is not out, and she is an ingénue."

"Do you think her unworthy of my attention?" The unmasked contempt in George's query caught her off guard, because she never once considered him in earnest. "Do you believe her unsuitable?"

"Of course, not." She smacked a fist to a palm. Oh, where was Mark when she needed him? "If I thought you pursued her, in truth, with honorable intentions, I should applaud your choice. But you will not dally with her heart, because it is wrong, and I adore her." Then she inclined her head and in a quiet voice asked, "Are you sincere?"

"That is ridiculous." He drained his glass and poured a refill. "Like Miss Logan, I have no wish to wed."

"But you will." She met his turbulent gaze. "And when you meet your special lady, you will know it, as sure as you know your name."

"Is that how you felt when you met Uncle Mark?" He stiffened his spine. "Because I heard he insulted you."

"Indeed, he did, but it did not matter." She recalled that magical if not so graceful introduction so long ago and clutched her clasped hands to her bosom. "I wish I could explain it in terms you could comprehend, but what I experienced at the Northcote's ball defies efforts to define it, and no mere words could describe it. Suffice it to say I knew, beyond all doubt, that Mark was fated to be mine, as I was his, and no one, not even my father, could convince me otherwise. Is that what you share with Eileen? Because if it is not, then you have no business seeking her company."

"I am truly sorry, Aunt Amanda." George speared his fingers through his hair, just as someone knocked at the door.

"Come." She whirled about to greet the untimely interloper.

"My lady." Hamilton bowed. "I apologize for intruding, but Viscount and Viscountess Wainsbrough, Sir Dalton and Mrs. Randolph, and Her Grace and Lady Beth are just arrived."

"Thank you, Hamilton. I will be right there." Amanda rolled her shoulders and caught George in her sights. "You were raised as a gentleman, and you know what is expected of you, so there will be no more kissing for you beneath my roof. Am I clear?"

Duly chastised, George dipped his chin. "Yes, Aunt Amanda."

CHAPTER FIVE

December 24, 1816

To Mark's unmitigated gratitude, the owner of the chicken farm maintained a small cabin for seasonal workers, near the hen houses, so he and Frederick enjoyed their own bunks and a relatively quiet accommodation, after the miserable sleigh ride. Fortunately for him, Cuthbert's cousin James planned a trip to Faversham the next day, because his wife had relations in the area, and they intended to spend the holidays with their family.

Sitting at a small table, he inhaled the scrambled eggs, toast, and kippers a charwoman delivered just after dawn, because James wanted to get an early start. For some reason Mark did not quite understand, the host suggested the journey to Faversham would take the entire day, when they should have made it in a couple of hours by coach.

"Oh, I forgot to mention I borrowed a blade, if you want to shave." Frederick drained his cup of tea and wiped his mouth. "You know, for the first time since we commenced this nightmare of a trip, I actually feel human after that marvelous hot bath. And I am thrilled that we do not have to ride a horse to get you home, because my arse still smarts. Now, if only I had a change of clothes, I should celebrate, but I suppose we had to leave our trunks with your man, because we could not carry them. By the by, you have a boney arse."

"See? Things are getting better, and I acknowledge your criticism, but my Amanda has no complaints, and she is all that matters." Mark stood and walked to the washstand. "And we will soon be home." Something occurred to him as he grabbed the soap. "What of your parents? And do you not have two sisters? They cannot all be gone. Why do you not celebrate Christmastide with them?"

"Life happened, Mark." Frederick tried in vain to smooth the wrinkles from his coat. "While you and I sailed the seas and climbed the ranks of the Royal Navy, life happened without us, and we cannot change it. For some, upon return, what remained of their world included no place for them, and it is just as well."

"But you can go home and visit, can you not?" Mark worked up a thick lather and smeared it over his skin. In the mirror, he monitored his handiwork as he shaved and tried not to reflect on the worry his wife, no doubt, suffered. There would be hell to pay, but he would gladly do her bidding to pass the night in her arms. "Do they still reside in Portsmouth, or was it Plymouth?"

"Plymouth." Frederick stacked the dishes and folded the cloth napkins. "There is still some tea in the pot, if you want it."

"No, thank you." Mark rinsed and dried his face. After kissing the portrait miniature of his bride, he tucked it, along with her handkerchief, in the little pocket of his waistcoat and donned his coat. "I say, did not your elder sister marry a lobster? As I recall, he was a lieutenant assigned to the *Inconstant*, was he not?"

"Yes." Frederick folded the blanket from his bunk. "What of it?"

"I was just wondering—"

"*Oy.*" James opened the door to the cabin, and Mark turned. "Admirals, we are ready to depart, if you will join us in the yard."

"I am only too delighted." He held the oak panel for his friend and followed him outside, where a large cart awaited, and he halted in his tracks, as his stomach sank. Frederick would never forgive Mark. "Hell and the Reaper."

"You are going to pay for this," Frederick whispered. "And I am not talking about something as simple as brandy and cigars."

"I could not have possibly known." Mark reminded himself of his predicament, and he was in no position to be choosy. "But it may not be that bad."

"Since I have to go to Faversham, I figured I would work along the way." Without a care, James lifted his wife, who carried a small babe, to the seat. "Just jump in the back, and make yourselves comfortable, because we have several stops to make, given I have numerous orders to fill."

So that was why the relatively short journey would take all day.

"Right." Mark offered Frederick a hand, but he slapped him aside.

"I can do it myself." With a wild series of grunts, in perfect time with multiple failed leaps, Frederick gained the cart with a healthy push from Mark. "Where are we to sit?"

"Anywhere there is room," James replied. "And hurry it up, because I would like to make Faversham by nightfall."

"Nightfall?" Frederick remarked in a high-pitched tone, as his eyes widened. "And what a lovely smell you have discovered."

"Stop grousing." Mark climbed into the not-so-elegant rig and shoved aside a crate. "Would you rather walk?"

"Yes." A chicken clucked a response, and Frederick rolled his eyes. "And I thought it could not get worse."

"My friend, if there is anything we learned in the navy, it is that it can always get worse." Tucked amid stacks and stacks of foul fowl, Mark and Frederick held fast, as James barked a command, and the cart pitched and lurched into motion. After navigating the farm road, the cart turned onto the lane with a mighty jolt, which thrust Frederick at Mark. "Really, though, it is somewhat comfortable, and the birds deflect some of the wind."

"Keep telling yourself that, because you just might believe it." Frederick shook his head. Somewhere in the heap a rooster crowed. "Oh, shut up."

∽

CHRISTMAS EVE WAS ALWAYS a calamitous affair in the Douglas household. With the entire Brethren family gathered in the drawing room, Amanda sat in a high back chair near the window, bouncing Horatio in her lap and searching through the snow for any sign of Mark.

"Lady Amanda, would you care for more tea?" Red-faced and sporting puffy eyes, as if from crying, Eileen dragged a chair near the hearth. "Or, perhaps, some company?"

"They can be a bit overwhelming, but you will accustom yourself to them." Amanda tittered, as Weston, Trevor's heir, rode Blake's back, and Edward, Everett's heir, mounted his papa and charged with great fanfare. "And I hope my nephew did not ruin your holiday. George is a nice boy, if only he remembers that."

"But Viscount Huntingdon's behavior does not signify, Lady Amanda." Despite evidence to the contrary, Eileen projected a shaky smile. "His was harmless banter and play, and I apologize if I concerned you."

"Nonsense, my dear." In that moment, Amanda noted George's attention focused on Eileen, and she arched a brow. Despite the protests, there were games afoot, and she met Hamilton's stare.

"Yes, my lady?" The butler clasped his hands behind his back. "How may I be of service?"

"Send for the nannies, as it is time for the children to retire." Shuffling Horatio, she bent her head and kissed his temple. "We should bring in the Yule Log, because the carolers will soon arrive to serenade us."

Given that was always Mark's task, she swallowed the bitter pill of disappointment as she issued orders to the Brethren. Again, she glanced out the window, as the sun set on the horizon and nightfall encroached with still no word of her husband.

"Allow me." Dirk passed Angeline to Rebecca and elbowed his sibling. "Dalton, give me a hand."

"Aye, brother." Dalton saluted and kissed Daphne. "I will be right back, darling."

"Mama, in light of Papa's absence, should we wait to exchange gifts when he returns?" Sabrina hugged her swollen belly and frowned. "Christmastide does not seem the same without my father in residence."

"My dear, I could not agree more." Fingering the expensive necklace at her throat, Amanda lamented Mark's empty chair, where they often spent lazy afternoons. "But he would not want us to forgo our customary celebrations on his account, so you may indulge as you see fit."

After the nannies collected the younger generation of Brethren, Amanda perused the tea trolley and the half-empty decanter of brandy. Given the servants busied themselves with various responsibilities, she decided to retrieve a bottle of the amber liquor from Mark's study.

As she strolled into the foyer, she spied the distinct glow of coach lights and shrieked. "It is Mark!"

Her shout of alarm brought the household running, and she yanked open the door without summoning the butler. The coach drew to a halt, as she descended the entrance stairs, and then she drew up short.

The rig was empty.

Biting the fleshy side of her hand, she sobbed.

"My lady." The coachman tipped his hat and jumped from the seat. "I have come to deliver the trunks."

"But—where is Admiral Douglas?" Choking on sheer terror, she fought tears. "Where is Mark?"

"The Admiral is not here?" The coachman blinked. "That is not possible, because he departed Dartford before I did, given I had to supervise repairs to the axle."

"Repairs?" She swallowed hard. "What happened to the axle?"

"I beg your pardon, my lady, but I thought you knew." As the footmen collected two trunks from the coach, Amanda waved the coachman inside, where it was warm. "So you have not seen Admiral Douglas or Admiral Maitland?"

"Clegg, you are the first to arrive, and I would have a full account of Admiral Douglas's whereabouts." In the foyer, she shut the door. Surrounded by her extended family, she resolved to remain calm, even as panic nipped at her heels. "Now, start at the beginning, and tell me everything."

Had she thought she was frightened?

As Clegg relayed the harrowing accident, Amanda clutched Cara's hand. To her relief, the coachman explained that Mark and his friend were not injured in the initial mishap, and for that she uttered a silent prayer of thanks. But when Clegg detailed Mark's departure, on horseback no less, she grew more concerned by the minute.

Where was her beloved husband?

"After the Admiral and Admiral Maitland made for Rochester, I engaged the services of a local builder to refit the axle and replace the broken wheels, and I resumed the journey yesterday." Clegg furrowed his brow and frowned. "I assumed they were here, my lady."

"We should form a search party," stated Blake in a grave voice. "They could be injured."

"The roads are too hazardous—you said so, yourself." Amanda considered the possibilities. "And Mark would not want you to risk your lives on his behalf, thus I will not allow it."

"My lady, this is my fault." Clegg bowed his head. "I will leave, at once, to find the Admiral."

"No, you will not." As much as she wanted to yield to his position, she could not, in good conscience, do so. "But you may depart at dawn, and retrace the journey, that you might locate Admiral Douglas. For now, I would have you take a hot meal and get some rest, which you have more than earned, that you may be awake and alert, tomorrow."

"Aye, my lady." Clegg bowed and exited.

When Amanda confronted her family, she noted the lines of strain and grim faces.

"What is this?" She clapped twice. "Dirk, I believe you were going to carry in the Yule Log." To Cara, Amanda said, "Dearest, would you be so good as to welcome the carolers, if I am not here to do so, as I left something in my chamber?"

"Of course, Mama." Cara sniffed and wiped a stray tear. "All right, everyone. Let us return to the drawing room."

Putting one foot in front of the other, Amanda climbed the grand staircase and crossed the gallery, blowing a kiss to Mark's resplendent portrait, in insouciant salute. In the hall that led to their private apartment, she relaxed her shoulders and inhaled a deep breath. After navigating their sitting room, she continued to the inner chamber, marching straight to his side of their bed. Sitting at the edge of the mattress, she pulled his pillow from beneath the covers, hugged it to her chest, opened the door to her heartache, and wept.

CHAPTER SIX

December 25, 1816

To Mark's abiding delight, when he exited the inn at Faversham on Christmas morning, he discovered the snow had finally stopped. Intent on walking home, which should have put his arrival at just past noon, he stamped his booted feet for warmth.

"Are you sure you do not want to try and find a ride the rest of the way?" Frederick slapped his forearms and shuddered, as an unrelenting gale whipped through the city. "You could stay here, with me. They have rooms aplenty."

"While I appreciate the offer, and it is tempting, given your amity, I must return to my Amanda." Although he would miss breakfast, if he were lucky, he might make the holiday meal, over which he always presided with his lady at his side. "As it stands, I am unforgivably late already, and—"

"*Admiral.*" A familiar shout snared Mark's attention, and he turned just as Clegg pulled the coach alongside the curb. "Admiral Douglas. Sir, thank heaven I found you."

"Clegg?" The coachman could have knocked Mark over with a feather. "How did you get here?"

"I found a smithy to repair the axle the day after you departed Dartford," Clegg explained, and then he detailed the refitting that allowed him to complete the journey. "When I discovered you were not in residence, I promised Her Ladyship that I would not return without you, Admiral."

"Do you mean to tell me that we would have arrived yesterday, had we remained with you, in Dartford?" Frederick asked with a vast deal of incredulity. "That we could have avoided the miserable trip?"

"So it seems, Admiral Maitland." Clegg snickered. "Now, shall we go, as Lady Amanda sits at the front window?"

"How is my wife?" Mark opened the door but paused. "Is she well?"

"My lady is worried, sir." Clegg's frown told Mark all he needed to know, and he jumped into the squabs.

"Are you sure you will not join me, Frederick?" Mark relished the heat of the small foot stove. "We have ample space, and you are quite welcome."

"Mark, I thank you." Frederick tipped his hat. "But I have a full belly, a comfortable bed, and I am warm. Indeed, I have everything I want, right here, so here I shall stay. And I bid you a Happy Christmas, old friend."

"And the same to you." Mark nodded once, closed the door, and pounded the side of the coach. "Drive on."

As the rig pulled into the lane, Mark replayed the somewhat hilarious chain of events that led him to that moment. He winced as he revisited the instant he discovered Frederick huddled to Mark's back. He snickered when he recalled Frederick bouncing in the saddle of that poor mare. He guffawed as he remembered the awkward sleigh ride spent in Frederick's lap. And then there were the chickens.

Indeed, it was quite an adventure—one he would never forget.

But then something struck him as odd. The underlying sadness. The solemnity. The proclamation that should have provoked suspicion that all was not as it appeared in Frederick's life.

While you and I sailed the seas and climbed the ranks of the Royal Navy, life happened without us, and we cannot change it. For some, upon return, what remained of their world included no place for them, and it is just as well.

"Oy, Clegg." Mark lowered the window and rapped on the coach door. "Turn around, and go back to the inn."

In mere minutes, the skilled coachman navigated the snow-covered road, and as the coach slowed, Mark leaped to the sidewalk. He burst through the door of the quaint establishment, glanced left and then right, and located Frederick nursing a glass of brandy and sitting at a table in the dining room.

"What happened to Abigail?" Mark asked in a quiet tone. "And why did you never marry her?"

"Because she died in childbirth," Frederick replied in a bare whisper that all but screamed agony. "Along with my heir."

"Why did you not tell me?" Mark eased to a chair opposite his friend. "And when did this occur?"

"While we patrolled the North Atlantic aboard the *Renegade*." A tear streamed his cheek, and he averted his stare. "And it is not the sort of thing one shares about the woman he loves, that he ruined her prior to speaking the vows because he could not resist her. That they yielded to the passion, which ended in death. Owing to my shame and the subsequent scandal that rocked Plymouth, my father banished me, and I have had no contact with my family, ever since. Of course, you would know naught of such things, given you lead the perfect life, but I never had your discipline, and I paid for it, in Abigail's blood."

"My friend, we are more alike than you realize, because Amanda was with child when we married, but to say more would be ungentlemanly." Mark grabbed the crystal balloon and downed the contents in a single gulp. "And we, too, lost our firstborn, after I left Amanda with the Siddons, in Jamaica, because she suffered the sickness. But a fever swept the island, and when I returned I found my wife deathly ill and the babe gone. That is why she sailed with me, thereafter. That is why we live in each other's pockets. And that is why I must get home to her, posthaste." He stood. "Now, get out of that chair, because you are not alone, and you are going to spend Christmastide with me and my family."

∿

CHRISTMASTIDE DAWNED on a blustery day with a cloud-filled sky, adequate to Amanda's mood. After dismissing her lady's maid, she checked her appearance in the long mirror. As per her custom, she boasted a gown of navy blue velvet festooned with the braided regalia of an admiral, to honor the love of her life, and told herself he would be there to savor her attire. Toying with the necklace of diamonds and sapphires, she closed her eyes and uttered a prayer for Mark's safe return.

In his dressing area, she smoothed the lapel of his coat of grey Bath superfine and then studied the new black waistcoat, which matched his breeches; she sewed just for the occasion. The shine on his boots reflected her image, meeting her strict specifications, and his lawn shirt and yard-length of linen were heavily starched.

If only Mark was there to wear the items.

"My darling, how I miss you." With a sigh, she strolled from their apartment and descended the staircase, to take her husband's place at the head of the table.

In the foyer, she peered out the side window. To her disappointment, there was no sign of the coach. As promised, Clegg departed early that morning, vowing to bring Mark home, and she requested the usual place settings, as she held out hope for his arrival.

"My lady, breakfast is served, and the family is gathered in the dining room." Hamilton then addressed the footman on guard. "Remember, you are to notify me, at once, if you spy the coach,"

"Yes, Mr. Hamilton." The footman nodded.

Reminding herself that she was the lady of the manor, Amanda squared her shoulders and strode to the dining room. When she entered, the men stood, and she waved. "Please, be seated, and let us enjoy the lovely meal I planned."

At the first pop of the cork, she recalled the morning toast Mark always offered, and she struggled to compose an elegant oratory, as she assumed his position. Something inside her fractured, as she caressed the stem of the elegant crystal, because, without Mark, everything was wrong.

Closing her eyes, she invoked his image, and he magically appeared before her, with his arms outstretched. Oh, his thick brown hair, which she often yanked in the throes of passion. His chiseled cheekbones. His patrician features. His blue eyes swimming with naughty thoughts. His stalwart frame. More than anything, she longed for his lips, which could kiss her into sweet oblivion, banishing the most grievous torment, and how she needed him.

"My lady." The plea came to her, as if from afar. "My lady."

Torn from the cherished respite, she shook herself and discovered Hamilton at her left. "Yes? What is it?"

"The footman observed the coach coming down the drive." The butler pulled back her chair, and she leaped to her feet.

In seconds, she sprinted into the foyer. Without donning her pelisse, she threw open the door, just as the coachman drew rein, and Mark jumped to the ground. With outstretched hands, he made for her, and she flew into his ready embrace.

Everything she held inside burst forth as a raging river, and she collapsed in a spate of tears, as she buried her face in the curve of his neck. For a while, Mark just stood there, rocking back and forth, while she wept.

"Darling, we have guests," he said at last, in a whisper.

"I know." Relaxing her grip, she slid down the front of him and wiped her eyes. Turning, she inhaled a calming breath. "Why, Admiral Maitland, what a wonderful surprise." When she cast a glance at Hamilton, he nodded and dispatched a footman, and she again addressed Maitland. "We are honored to have you with us."

"Lady Amanda." Maitland doffed his hat, took her hand in his, and pressed a chaste kiss to her knuckles. "The honor is mine."

"Please, come inside and take your ease. We were just about to sit down to breakfast." As she ushered Mark and his friend into the house, she peered over her shoulder, and to Clegg she mouthed, *Thank you*. To wit, he dipped his chin.

"Thank you, everyone, for the warm welcome, and it is good to be home." Swamped amid the Brethren, Mark reached for her. "Now, if you will assemble in the dining room, my lady and I will join you shortly."

To her surprise, while the family went one way, she and Mark went the other, as he drew her into his study. After he shut the door, he turned, and she found herself beset by six feet of aroused male.

"I know this dress, and more importantly the woman in it, and I see you got my gift." As he pressed her against the wall, he bent his head and trailed his tongue along her décolletage, and her knees buckled. "But I am in dire need of a bath, I need to visit our son, and then I need to spend the better part of an hour making love to my wife."

"You are late." She raked her nails along his nape.

"My Amanda, you are stunning, as always." To her abiding delight, he showered her face in kisses. "And I love you."

"You are forgiven." She giggled, as he nibbled the crest of her ear and fondled her bottom through the heavy velvet skirt. "What kept you from our bed, my darling?"

"A promotion and a series of events you may not believe." At last, he tightened an arm about her waist and cupped her cheek. "You are looking at the Royal Navy's First Sea Lord."

"Oh, Mark, I am so proud of you." It was her turn to kiss him, and she applied herself that he might have no doubt of her regard. "I shall commission a gown with the requisite regalia, *my lord*."

"What I would do to you, were we alone." He thrust his hips, as if she could possibly be oblivious to his desire. "But we have a house filled with family, and duty calls."

"Indeed, but you will not let that stop you, later." She straightened his cravat and then pulled a feather from his coat. "What is this?"

"It is a long story, which I will share, tonight." He laughed and then stood at attention. "Now, will the most beautiful Lady Amanda consent to escort this humble sailor to breakfast?"

"Oh, she will do more than that, my lord." Emboldened, she rubbed his crotch and whispered something naughty.

"Good lord, woman." Mark exhaled audibly. "Married thirty years, and you still make me tremble. Let us convene in the dining room, that we might celebrate our reunion in private."

Arm in arm, Mark and Amanda returned to the festivities and assumed their requisite places. After Hamilton dispensed the champagne, Mark held high his glass, and the gathering quieted.

In that peaceful calm, Amanda admired the large extended family comprised of colorful characters. The legacy of the Brethren manifested a fierce collective of daring Nautionnier Knights and the spirited women who claimed their hearts, along with an unshakable love independent of romance, which spanned the distance of time and place, never waning.

Constant as the rising sun, the bonds of kinship knew no price and made no demands. For such devotion existed in a realm unencumbered by envy or other human imperfections. Indeed, it burned as an eternal flame, to inspire future generations. When Mark clutched her hand in his, she knew, without doubt, he felt it, too.

"Friends and family, once again we are fortunate to rally for the holidays, and this Christmastide, as opposed to those of the past, has served to remind me of what is most important, so I shall keep my customary remarks brief." He squeezed her fingers and winked. "It is not the presents we exchange but the time we spend, together, that ranks supreme. It is not Stir-Up Day, the kissing bough, the Yule Log, the plum pudding, or the carolers but the giving of ourselves that truly exhibits the spirit of the season, and I may have forgot that until my most recent journey. But this morning, as I study your faces, I realize I am a fortunate man, thus I wish a Happy Christmas, to one and all."

THE END

You can learn more about the entire Brethren of the Coast series at barbaradevlin.com.

ABOUT BARBARA DEVLIN

A proud Latina, USA Today bestselling author Barbara Devlin was born a storyteller, but it was a weeklong vacation to Bethany Beach, Delaware that forever changed her life. The little house her parents rented had a collection of books by Kathleen Woodiwiss, which exposed Barbara to the world of romance, and *Shanna* remains a personal favorite.

Barbara writes heartfelt historical romances that feature not so perfect heroes who may know how to seduce a woman but know nothing of marriage. And she prefers feisty but smart heroines who sometimes save the hero before they find their happily ever after.

Barbara is a disabled-in-the-line-of-duty retired police officer, and she earned an MA in English and continued a course of study for a Doctorate in Literature and Rhetoric. She happily considered herself an exceedingly eccentric English professor, until success in Indie publishing lured her into writing, full-time, featuring her fictional knighthood, the Brethren of the Coast.

Connect with Barbara Devlin at BarbaraDevlin.com, where you can sign up for her newsletter, The Knightly News.

ALSO BY BARBARA DEVLIN

BRETHREN OF THE COAST

Loving Lieutenant Douglas

Enter the Brethren

My Lady, the Spy

The Most Unlikely Lady

One-Knight Stand

Captain of Her Heart

The Lucky One

Love with an Improper Stranger

To Catch a Fallen Spy

Hold Me, Thrill Me, Kiss Me

The Duke Wears Nada

A Very Brethren Christmas

Owner of a Lonely Heart

BRETHREN ORIGINS

Arucard

Demetrius

Aristide

Morgan

Geoffrey

PIRATES OF THE COAST

The Black Morass

The Iron Corsair

The Buccaneer

The Stablemaster's Daughter

The Marooner

Once Upon a Christmas Knight

The Reaper

WORLD OF DE WOLFE PACK

Lone Wolfe

The Big Bad De Wolfe

Tall, Dark & De Wolfe

MAGICK TRILOGY

Magick, Straight Up

A Taste of Magick

Magick in the Air

PIRATES OF BRITANNIA

The Blood Reaver

THE MAD MATCHMAKING MEN OF WATERLOO

The Accidental Duke

The Accidental Groom

Made in the USA
Middletown, DE
17 May 2025